Praise for *The First Christmas*

"I love *The First Christmas*. What a charming way Stephen Mitchell has found to tell my favorite story of all, the Nativity, character by character (I love the donkey and the ox), with wise and thrilling interludes about God, reality, truth."

—Anne Lamott, author of *Bird by Bird*

"*The First Christmas* is a wonderful book, tender and rich with bursts of humor, filled with curious contrivances and surprises. Reading it felt like opening a brightly wrapped Christmas present and finding a second box (also brightly wrapped) inside, and inside *that* box a third, and then another, and another, and another. Until, at the very center, in a tiny box, there is a diamond: the wisdom contained within this telling."

—Elizabeth Gilbert, author of *Eat Pray Love*

"Stephen Mitchell's *The First Christmas* is a wholly original and deeply inspired book. I'm swept away by his language: simple and concrete, fetching. Mitchell grants us access here to the kingdom of heaven that lies within us, folded in a simple story."

—Jay Parini, author of *Jesus: The Human Face of God*

"As he has done before to our enlightenment and delight, Stephen Mitchell takes an ancient text and opens it and illuminates it for our time. And now, the Nativity story! Who knew there were so many perspectives from ox to innkeeper, shepherds to seekers, to Mitchell himself—all helping us see this seminal event in heartwarming, eye-opening complexity and compassion. As is often said about an important and riveting and life-changing event: you had to be there. In *The First Christmas*, Mitchell puts us there, and the birth and rebirth happen in the reader as well—no matter how well we know the story. Mitchell's illumined text is a star that leads us to a new understanding of the Bethlehem moments in our lives." —Julia Alvarez, author of
How the García Girls Lost Their Accents
and *In the Time of the Butterflies*

The First Christmas

By Stephen Mitchell

POETRY AND FICTION
The First Christmas • *The Way of Forgiveness* • *The Frog Prince* • *Meetings with the Archangel* • *Parables and Portraits*

NONFICTION
A Mind at Home with Itself (with Byron Katie) • *A Thousand Names for Joy* (with Byron Katie) • *Loving What Is* (with Byron Katie) • *The Gospel According to Jesus*

TRANSLATIONS AND ADAPTATIONS
Beowulf • *The Odyssey* • *The Iliad* • *Duino Elegies & The Sonnets to Orpheus* • *The Second Book of the Tao* • *Gilgamesh* • *Bhagavad Gita* • *Full Woman, Fleshly Apple, Hot Moon: Selected Poems of Pablo Neruda* • *Genesis* • *Ahead of All Parting: The Selected Poetry and Prose of Rainer Maria Rilke* • *A Book of Psalms* • *The Selected Poetry of Dan Pagis* • *Tao Te Ching* • *The Book of Job* • *The Selected Poetry of Yehuda Amichai* (with Chana Bloch) • *The Lay of the Love and Death of Cornet Christoph Rilke* • *Letters to a Young Poet* • *The Notebooks of Malte Laurids Brigge* • *The Selected Poetry of Rainer Maria Rilke* • *T. Carmi and Dan Pagis: Selected Poems*

EDITED BY STEPHEN MITCHELL

Question Your Thinking, Change the World: Quotations from Byron Katie • *The Essence of Wisdom* • *Bestiary: An Anthology of Poems about Animals* • *Song of Myself* • *Into the Garden: A Wedding Anthology* (with Robert Hass) • *The Enlightened Mind: An Anthology of Sacred Prose* • *The Enlightened Heart: An Anthology of Sacred Poetry* • *Dropping Ashes on the Buddha: The Teaching of Zen Master Seung Sahn*

FOR CHILDREN

The Ugly Duckling, by Hans Christian Andersen • *Iron Hans* • *Genies, Meanies, and Magic Rings* • *The Tinderbox, by Hans Christian Andersen* • *The Wishing Bone and Other Poems* • *The Nightingale, by Hans Christian Andersen* • *Jesus: What He Really Said and Did* • *The Creation*

✱

The First Christmas

A STORY OF
NEW BEGINNINGS

Stephen Mitchell

ST. MARTIN'S
ESSENTIALS
NEW YORK

First published in the United States by St. Martin's Essentials, an imprint of St. Martin's Publishing Group

Designed by Steven Seighman

A brief portion of this book has been adapted from *Meetings with the Archangel*, New York: HarperCollins, 1998.

"The Well Dressed Man with a Beard" from *The Collected Poems of Wallace Stevens* copyright © 1954 by Wallace Stevens and copyright renewed 1982 by Holly Stevens. Used by permission of Alfred A. Knopf, an imprint of the Knopf Doubleday Publishing Group, a division of Penguin Random House LLC. All rights reserved.

The Library of Congress has cataloged the hardcover edition as follows:

Names: Mitchell, Stephen, 1943– author.
Title: The first Christmas : a story of new beginnings / Stephen Mitchell.
Description: First edition. | New York : St. Martin's Essentials, 2021. |
    Includes bibliographical references.
Identifiers: LCCN 2021016079 | ISBN 9781250790699 (hardcover) |
    ISBN 9781250790705 (ebook)
Subjects: LCSH: Jesus Christ—Nativity—Fiction. | GSAFD: Bible fiction.
Classification: LCC PS3563.I8235 F57 2021 | DDC 813/.6—dc23
LC record available at https://lccn.loc.gov/2021016079

First Edition: 2021

10 9 8 7 6 5 4 3 2 1

To Katie

Christ's birth is always happening. And yet if it doesn't happen in me, how can it help me? Everything depends on that.

—MEISTER ECKHART

At the Passover seder, a Hasidic rabbi told his chief disciple to go outside and see if the Messiah had come. "But Rabbi," the disciple said, pointing to his heart, "if the Messiah has come, wouldn't you know it in here?" "Ah," said the rabbi, pointing to his own heart. "In here, the Messiah has already come."

Contents

Foreword

I N WRITING THIS BOOK, I wanted to see where the givens of the Nativity story would lead. My only agenda was to inhabit the characters. I hope that I've done this in a way that is respectful to Christians, but I have written for Jews and Muslims as well and for secular readers who find meaning and delight in the story. The beauty of the traditional narrative is self-evident in the annunciation to Mary,* the triumph over jealousy and distrust that Joseph must achieve, all the beloved details of the Nativity scene—the snow (not in the Gospels), the ox and donkey (ditto), the star (Matthew), the angels (Luke), the shepherds (Luke) and wise men (Matthew): the poetry of a new beginning, when winter turns toward the sun, and

---

* I call the principal characters by the Aramaic names they would have used themselves: Maryam (Mār'yam, accent on the first syllable; rhymes with "far calm") and Yosef (Yō'sef).

the joy of an imagined child who, in the words of Isaiah, is given to us all.

Like every magical tale, this one asks us to temporarily suspend our disbelief and expand our imaginations. Jews and atheists will need to accept the angelic visit and the virginal conception as givens of the story. Christians will need to take a leap of unfaith, over the Christology of the early Church, and place themselves inside the minds of Jewish characters living in the year 4 BCE, fifty-five years before the earliest Christian texts were written.* There would have been no way for a historical Mary or Joseph to make sense of religious concepts like Jesus as the preexisting third person of the Trinity or as a savior who by his sacrificial death atones for the sins of those who believe in him. "Messiah" would have meant one thing only: the fully human being, announced by the prophets, whose kingship would bring complete and lasting peace to the earth. In the same way, the

---

* The earliest is the First Epistle to the Thessalonians, which dates from about 51 CE. The earliest Gospel, the Gospel According to Mark, was probably written between 65 and 70. Matthew's Gospel probably dates from 80 to 85 and Luke's from 85 to 90. (John's, the latest Gospel, written around the year 100, has almost nothing to do with the historical Jesus.)

phrase "son of God" would have meant either a Jewish king or a righteous man; the Christian concept of an "only begotten son" would have seemed obscene and pagan to any Jew and profoundly disrespectful, if not insane.

I have imagined Mary as a very young woman in love with her future husband. Christian tradition turns Joseph into an old man, so that Mary's love for him might have nothing sexual about it, and it sees Mary as a proto-nun who has taken a vow of perpetual virginity, though for a pious Jewish girl such a vow would have been unthinkable, since it would transgress God's commandment to be fruitful and multiply. But the Gospel stories say nothing about Joseph's age. As a man about to be married, he would probably be in his early or mid twenties. If Mary loves him and wants to have his children (later they have six children together),* then the announcement that she is to get pregnant without him, by the Holy Spirit descending on her, would at first seem appalling.

Mary would also be aware of her beloved's probable reaction to the news that she is pregnant, not to

---

* Mark 6:3.

speak of the reaction of the whole village. It would form the background to her yes: the prospect of universal contempt—of being seen by everyone she loved and by everyone else as a whore. "The angel," Søren Kierkegaard astutely pointed out, "didn't appear to the other young girls in Israel and say, 'Don't despise Mary; the extraordinary is happening to her.' No, the angel came to Mary alone, and no one was able to understand her. Has any woman ever been as humiliated as Mary was, and isn't it true here that the one God blesses He curses in the same breath? This is the spirit's view of Mary, and she is not—it is revolting that I have to say this, but it is even more revolting that people have thoughtlessly and sanctimoniously depicted her in this way—she is not a lady lounging in fancy dress and playing with an infant god."

You may also be surprised that in my Nativity scenes there is little focus on the baby. We usually imagine the Nativity through the filter of Christian iconography, in which the divine child is the cynosure of neighboring eyes, worshiped by humans and angels. But for Jewish characters like my shepherds and wise men, worshiping a human being would be sheer paganism. Their focus would be on what the child is about to bring to the world, on the world he is about to bring into existence, not on the child himself.

Mary and Joseph are, of course, at the center of the story. Each one ends up acting with a moral courage that is beyond praise. It is their courage that makes the spirit of Christmas possible.

1

The Innkeeper

Jove nods to Jove from behind each of us.

—EMERSON

I T WAS SNOWING AGAIN as they arrived, the man and the girl. They had been on the road for six days, traveling fifteen miles a day except when she felt too unwell to continue. The man went on foot, leading the donkey. The girl on the donkey was wrapped in an extra cloak that covered her head, her back, and her swollen belly. Much of the time she barely noticed the road they were traveling on. Her attention was focused on the child inside her, and she would track its movements with a fascinated delight. Sometimes she would talk to it or sing it a lullaby.

They had tried to find lodging at four inns already, but Bethlehem was swarming with pilgrims who had gathered there for the census. Half the population of the country, it seemed, were scions of the house of David; since the official genealogies had been destroyed six hundred years before, during the conquest of Jerusalem and the Babylonian captivity, anyone could assert that he was of royal blood, however down-at-heel he might look. The inns were full. Again and again the man had been turned away, each time with a brusque no. Now night was falling.

The innkeeper—a burly man in his forties with a tangled brown beard and a diagonal scar over his left eyebrow—told them they would have to wait, he would get to them as soon as he could; he was very busy, with a dozen requests to attend to. All the rooms were occupied, some of them with double or triple the usual number of guests, and the broad covered court-yard was so packed with bodies that he had to thread his way among them in order to bring someone wine or food. It took all his expertise to make his guests comfortable, or not overly uncomfortable. His wife and their two sons and three daughters were just as busy. It had been this way for weeks.

An hour later, when he returned to them, he paused to take a better look. The girl seemed to be fourteen or fifteen years old, and she was very pregnant. She stood with modestly downcast eyes, but beneath the shawl, enough of her face was visible that he could see how pretty she was: fine features, the nose delicately arched, the lips full and shapely, though chapped by the bitter cold. She was wearing a roughly woven light-brown woolen tunic that fell to her ankles and over it a cloak dyed a slightly darker brown. The man was in his twenties, of average height, about five feet four, heavy boned, with large hands and a full, reddish-brown beard. He was dressed in the same kind of tunic, which came to his knees and was fastened at the waist by a thick leather belt. His cloak reached midcalf and had the prescribed tassels at its four corners.

It turned out to be one more hard-luck story, as the innkeeper had suspected. He had heard many during the previous weeks. Royal descendants had asked him for a deduction in the price or suggested that he waive the price entirely, given the honor they were bestowing on him by their mere presence. Some of them, with tears in their eyes, had traced the downward descent of their family over the past six centuries. Some had paraded their grimy children before him and begged for his indulgence.

Given all his pressing obligations, he felt tempted to shoo the young couple away. He could do only so much, and in good conscience he wouldn't squeeze one more person into the already dangerously over-crowded courtyard. He wasn't God, after all, who could create something out of nothing. He was only a decent man trying to do his best in a situation that would have tested the patience of Job. No, they would have to be on their way. He was about to say this when something stopped him.

What was it? The young man looked composed, but it was obvious how weary he and the girl were and how close she was to giving birth. That wasn't *his* problem, of course, and he brushed away the brief thought of responsibility. But there was something in the young man's demeanor—a forthrightness, a sincerity—that touched his heart. "Is there no place at all for us?" The voice was calm and manly. There was no pleading in the tone, no attempt to persuade him or appeal to his sense of pity. As he looked into the young man's eyes, he felt as though a current of sympathy had somehow established itself between them. He was embarrassed by this; it was bad business practice. But he had to ac-knowledge it. A decision had been made somewhere inside him—in spite of him or without his conscious assent. They could stay.

But how? There was certainly no room for them,

and he couldn't ask any of his guests to leave. Suddenly an image arose in his mind, of the small, dilapidated stable in back of the inn, with its four narrow stalls and its single inhabitant, an ox that he rented to farmers during the season of plowing. The stable's roof was damaged, and there were loose stones on two of its sides, but it would provide shelter for the young couple. No time for thanks; they must follow him, quickly.

He threw a second cloak over his shoulders, lit a torch, and walked outside with them. Their small gray donkey was tethered to one of the posts in front of the inn. Snow covered her back and neck. When she saw them, she uttered a bray that was like a pump gone dry. The girl undid the rope and walked behind the two men with quick steps, hurrying to stay inside the circle of torchlight.

The stable smelled of straw and manure. Flies congregated in the ox's stall, crawled over the piles of dung, and reconnoitered on the walls. There were shallow stone troughs in each of the four stalls and enough clean straw to make beds for two people. The innkeeper placed the torch in the rusted iron holder on the wall, said good night, and was out the door, not even stopping long enough to listen to their thanks.

When the door closed, the man led the donkey into the stall next to the ox's. He put hay in the trough and a bucket of water beside it. (He had to break through the ice on its surface.) Then he undid his traveling sack and walked across to the stall they had chosen as their living quarters. By the time he got there, the girl was fast asleep.

Interlude

T HERE IS NO INNKEEPER in Luke's version of the Nativity story—just the very moving statement that Mary wrapped the baby in swaddling clothes and laid him in a manger, because there was no room for them at the inn. But if there is an inn, there must be an innkeeper. And why not imagine him as generously as possible—as not harshly turning the young couple away but doing the best he can? I feel great affection for this man, who in spite of himself does the right thing, for the right reason.

In an archetypal story, as in a dream, you are each one of the characters. Can you find your way into the innkeeper? It's probably easy to remember a time when you felt too busy to listen to someone in need. It may be more difficult to locate an experience when there was a current of sympathy between you and a complete stranger. But this happens to everyone. Some kind of decision has been made, even against your conscious will.

What made the decision? This is as fundamental a question as "Who am I?" There's no answer outside the question. But if you penetrate deeply enough, you'll see very clearly that you are not the doer, as the Bhagavad Gita helpfully points out. The innkeeper was an ordinary man, but perhaps after the fruitful chaos of the census had died down and all the pilgrims had departed and left Bethlehem the small sleepy town it had been, he remembered the moment when something beyond himself had made him extraordinary.

2

The Ox

Thou shalt not muzzle the ox.

—DEUTERONOMY 25:4

THOUGH I AM SOMEONE who enjoys his solitude, I am a sociable fellow by nature. Happiness loves company, as they say misery does. So when my master opened the door and brought in two humans and a donkey, I was delighted. I lowed with pleasure. This may have seemed rude, but I couldn't help it.

My master was out the door in a trice, letting in another blast of cold air. The man paused for a few moments, then brought the donkey into the stall next to mine and walked back to the woman. I poked my head over the partition to get a better look at my new neighbor. She was a jenny with a coat of lovely light-gray hair, quite young—five years old was my guess—and nine or ten hands high, which is on the short side for our region. She seemed friendly enough. She lifted her head toward me, and we touched muzzles in fellowship. But she was obviously exhausted, and after that brief acknowledgment she moved over to a corner of the stall, lay down, and fell asleep. Donkeys have the reputation of being temperamentally difficult, but I have never found that to be so. Of course, I have never plowed with one of them, since that is forbidden by law. But I have seen quite a few pass through the inn during my many years here, and on the whole they have seemed to me exemplary creatures: patient, industrious, and uncomplaining.

Now some of you, I am sure, assume that my attitude toward donkeys would be rather condescending. I would be entitled to that, you think, because first of all I am so much bigger and second, even more importantly, I am kosher and they are not, since they neither have cloven hoofs nor chew the cud. But you would be jumping to an unjustified conclusion. I pride myself on my tolerance. I am large not only in body but also in mind, and I believe I am being accurate in stating that I have never held a prejudice against unclean animals. As a matter of fact, the issue of ritual cleanness doesn't enter my consideration at all when I judge someone's character. I can think of a number of particularly foolish cows and sheep that I have turned up my muzzle at, while on the other hand some of my fondest acquaintanceships have been formed with donkeys and with the occasional camel or dromedary who has lodged here. (I haven't met any pigs, but I like to believe that I could keep an open mind even toward them, despite their appalling reputation.)

I couldn't help thinking what a pity it is that donkeys have never learned to chew the cud—nor have humans, for that matter. It's difficult for me to imagine what life must be like without it. Extremely stressful, I would think. We ruminative animals have been particularly blessed in our capacity for calm deliberation, and I have often thought that this is what distinguishes us, in terms of spiritual maturity, from other creatures. If you spend many hours a day chewing things over—not just reflecting on the events of your day but breaking them down into their constituent parts and truly digesting them—there is not much in life that can disturb you. People say that in India we are worshiped as gods or as manifestations of the supreme Lord. This should surprise no one, since India is a land of great spirituality, and it is only natural that humans who meditate should honor animals who ruminate. In any case, whether or not our spiritual qualities are recognized, we are, generally speaking, as mature a species as any I have encountered. Humans can be cruel, camels foul tempered, sheep flighty, donkeys raucous, horses high-strung, and pigs … well, I won't even go there. But there are no creatures so dependably placid in any contingency as we oxen are.

Now it is true that bulls have a justifiably mixed reputation. If you get a bull riled up, beware! But you must understand that bulls have a difficult set of expectations superimposed on their essentially peaceful nature. They know that their livelihood and their very existence depend on their ability to generate offspring. If they fall short, the ax awaits them, and the butcher's block. And with all that testosterone coursing through their limbs, it's no wonder that they can be aggressive when challenged. Every day I thank my lucky stars that I was castrated in my youth and was spared not just the impulse toward dominance but every kind of sexual frenzy. All that snorting and bellowing and pawing and thrusting: who would want to live a life of such unremitting ego? Of course, bulls would be far worse off if they didn't have their cud-chewing to fall back on. I am not trying to malign them—on the contrary. To my mind, however, the combination of great physical strength and sustained calm is something that belongs only to the ox, and in my humble opinion, as the epitome of imperturbability, we are one of the sovereign miracles of God's creation.

But I digress. I stood watching the jenny as she slept, and I watched the two humans, and I thought how cozy it was to ruminate inside the stable with my new neighbors. There was hardly a sound—just some rustling of the straw across the aisle and the snow falling steadily and softly on the roof. Then the rustling stopped. The humans were asleep, the donkey was asleep, and only I was left to watch over them. I chewed my cud slowly, savoring the ambrosial paste, and in the torchlight I could see the clouds of my breath float up and disperse in the frigid air. And so it continued for an hour or two. A pleasant, uneventful night, I thought: a silent night, a night of companionable peace. But what can we ever know? If I have learned anything during my many years of contemplation, it is that the future always eludes our grasp. Sometimes a surprise is waiting for us at the emptiest corner of the field.

And what a surprise this was! All at once the

woman began moaning. I recognized that sound. It was not a distress call exactly but the sound of great effort and pain. Before I came to live here, I lodged in a stable with many cows, ewes, and nannies, and I heard hundreds of births take place. The memories came back to me in a flash. Those pitiable moos, bleats, and baas were like the sounds the woman was making: the price of motherhood. I am grateful that I never had to go through that kind of pain myself, but what male could be so insensitive as not to feel his heart quiver in sympathy? I expected the woman to be finished in less than an hour, as with the births I had witnessed, but the moaning and screaming lasted much longer than that. The man sat beside her, wiping her brow, holding her in his arms, talking to her, singing to her. His voice was deep and comforting.

Finally, she pushed her child out into the world. It was a tiny creature, its skin dark red, almost purple. For a few moments I was concerned that it might not be breathing, but even as I chewed on that thought, the child broke into a lusty howl. The man picked it up and held it to the woman's breast. I was sorry to see that neither of them licked its body clean; but oh well, human ways are not our ways. The child continued to wail. After fifteen minutes or so it wore itself out, poor thing, and fell asleep.

I had never seen a human birth before, and this one moved me deeply. The donkey saw it too; she had found it impossible to stay asleep amid the uproar. So the two of us watched the two of them, and then we watched the three of them. I don't know what the donkey was feeling; she knew the man and the woman far better than I did, of course, but I can't imagine anyone being happier for them than I was. Joy took the shape of my body and filled it from my hoofs out to my tail and the tips of my horns.

There is an old prophecy among the humans here that someday there will be no more suffering in the world. There will be neither predators nor prey: wolves will dwell in peace with lambs, lions will eat hay just as we oxen do, leopards will lie down with kids and not ever be tempted to turn on them with their murderous teeth and claws. Personally, I can't imagine how this will happen; lions, for example, don't have the internal organs that would allow them to digest hay. But people say that what seems impossible to us creatures is possible for God. They also say that a little child will lead the wolves and lambs, the leopards and kids, the calves and the lions. I would like to see that parade. I would like to meet that child.

Perhaps someday, in spite of common sense, it will happen. In the meantime, I am glad that God has given me two sharp horns. I feel very protective toward the child who was born here tonight. If wolves or lions come here to harm him, I will chase them away, peaceable fellow though I am. I will stand in front of the child with lowered head to show them that I mean business. If they come any closer, I will gore them and toss them over my shoulders. No one will harm this child—not if I have anything to do with it.

Interlude

I T'S PROBABLY UNNECESSARY to mention this, but I have now stepped out of the ox and back into the authorial "I." I do this with no regrets, but I must tell you that I felt very comfortable as an ox. His mixture of intense solidity and immovable calm is something I know well. And the flavor of pride? I can find that too in myself. Whether it is as charming in me as it is in him is an open question.

He is, as I am, a peaceable fellow. But those horns he's provided with—he knows instinctively how to use them. Here too I can find the equivalent in myself, though I have used mine only once, in defending a principle. To my great surprise, I enjoyed using them. Actually, it was fascinating to face the rogue matador, then gore and toss him. (This metaphor is getting out of hand.)

But enough about me for the moment.

How does the present chapter connect to the Nativity story? Well, the ox was a given, since he's part of our folkloric legacy. His messianic musings are another connection. He is open to all possibilities, as anyone with a Whitmanesque largeness of mind would naturally be. But he is rightly skeptical of Isaiah's promise that the wild will be domesticated someday. I too can imagine a world in which our equivalent of swords have been transformed into our equivalent of plowshares. But lions eating hay? Wolves dwelling with lambs? Not going to happen, nor should it. Would you want the magnificent, dangerous world of nature to become a Disney cartoon in which bluebirds circle about your head, while serape-clad squirrels serenade you in the shade? The vision that came to Isaiah out of his great longing is not something any mature person would want to see realized.

What we long for in the outer world we can have within us, as Meister Eckhart and the Hasidic rabbi quoted at the beginning of this book realized. When the inner Messiah comes, we don't need an outer one.

3

The Shepherds

The humble will see this and be glad.

—PSALM 69:32

1.

THEY WERE PASTURING THEIR SHEEP on the hills outside Bethlehem. The flock didn't belong to them; it
belonged to a prosperous merchant who lived in Jerusalem. It numbered 227 sheep and lambs. They
knew the name of each one.

Three of the men were awake. The others had
gone off to sleep in the tent on the other side of the
hill. They would be coming back at the beginning
of the third watch, so that everyone could have six
hours' sleep. It had snowed heavily the day before,
and the ground was still white. The sheep had to

poke down through that layer to get at the remnants of grass. When they raised their heads in the starlight, snow clung to their muzzles.

Each of the shepherds was wrapped in a sheepskin cloak with the fleece turned inward. They were watching the sheep from within an oblong circle of stones. At the center of the circle was a fire and around it a layer of rushes on which the men sat or reclined. There was also a makeshift table—a flat log with half a loaf of wheat bread on it, along with some olives, dried fruit, and cheese. One shepherd played on his reed pipe, repeating the same tune over and over. From time to time, one of the others would leap up, run to the edge of the field, and toss a stone with his slingshot to frighten a sheep back into the flock or to drive off a prowling jackal.

Suddenly an angel appeared at the edge of the circle. His body seemed to be lit from the inside. The shepherds were startled; then they felt afraid. The angel was tall and had fiery red hair and a red beard. His face didn't look young, but it was unwrinkled and as white as the snow on the ground. He stood there and stared at them. His eyes never blinked.

Then the whole hillside lit up. The light was more brilliant than the sun's. They couldn't tell where it came from. Nothing around them cast a shadow. Their limbs began to tremble. The shepherd who had been playing the reed pipe burst into tears, then all three threw themselves onto the ground and covered their heads with their hands.

"Don't be afraid," the angel said. His voice was like music. Instantly each of them felt at ease. The trembling stopped, and they sat up to listen to his words with their mouths wide open. "I bring you good news of a great joy, which will happen for all the people. To you there is born this day, in the city of David, a child who is the Messiah. And this will be your sign: You will find the child wrapped in swaddling clothes, lying in a manger."

He stopped speaking, and for a moment there was a stunned silence. Then a voice came down to them from the North Star. It sang a single note of joy, but in that note all other notes were contained, as all colors are contained in white light. Then another note came down from another star, and another, and another, until the whole sky was filled with the music of hundreds upon hundreds of stars, each note blending into the harmony of all the others, each star scintillating with its own particular joy. The three shepherds watched and listened in wonder. At first the music was wordless, then the notes had words to them or they were also words. "Glory to God in the highest heavens," the stars sang, "and on earth peace, good will toward men."

Then the stars were silent. The angel was gone.

The three shepherds took a deep breath (they had barely been breathing, though they didn't know it) and looked at one another in astonishment.

The shepherd who had been playing on the reed pipe said in an awed whisper, as though to himself: "The Messiah has been born."

"In Bethlehem! Right here!" said a second shepherd. "Can you believe it?"

The third shepherd, who was much younger than the other two, said, "What does it mean?"

First shepherd: "What does it mean?! Don't be silly! Everyone knows what it means."

Second shepherd: "It means peace on earth, finally, after all this time. Didn't you hear what the stars were singing? 'On earth peace, good will toward men.'"

Third shepherd: "Oh. The words *I* heard were: 'On earth peace toward men of good will.'"

First shepherd: "Well, it's the same thing, since most of us Jews *are* men of good will. We're going to have peace in the Holy Land! No more Romans. No more Herod. The son of David will rule over us. Everyone will be happy. That's the good news. It's the best possible news."

Third shepherd: "But we *are* happy. What could be better than being a shepherd?"

Second shepherd: "Well, yes, but maybe now we'll have our own flock."

First shepherd: "No, no, that's not the point! I don't care *who* owns the flock. But when the Messiah comes, it will all be different. Don't you see? There won't be any sickness! That's what the prophets said. No more sheep dying of fever or bluetongue or bloat. No more ewes aborting or lambs going lame. We'll be spared all that heartache."

Third shepherd: "Ah. Wouldn't *that* be nice!"

Second shepherd: "And not only that. There won't be any more wolves or jackals! We won't need our slingshots anymore, except to tidy up the flock's edges."

First shepherd: "No, that's not what the prophets said—at least, that's not what *I've* heard. It's not that there won't be any wolves or jackals. It's just that they won't eat sheep. They'll eat grass, along with the lambs. They'll be tame, just like dogs. They'll come up to you, and you'll be able to pat them and scratch their heads. Maybe they'll even chase after sticks."

Third shepherd [*laughing*]: "That would be something! A wolf rolling over and wanting you to rub its belly."

First shepherd: "Or sitting up on its hind legs to beg for food. And you'll give it a big handful of grass."

Second shepherd: "Here, boy! Here, boy!"

The shepherds all laughed.

Third shepherd: "But why did the man say we're supposed to look for a baby?"

First shepherd: "He wasn't a man. He was an angel."

Third shepherd: "He was? Where were his wings?"

Second shepherd: "Wings? Don't be silly. Didn't you see his face? Nobody's skin is as white as that. And when did you ever see someone that big? He must have been six feet tall!"

Third shepherd: "Oh."

First shepherd: "He was like the angels who appeared to our father Abraham by the terebinths of Mamre. *They* didn't have wings. They sat down at his table, and the three of them ate a whole roast calf. They had healthy appetites, those angels."

Third shepherd: "But why did he come to *us*?

We're not holy like Abraham. We're just simple folk. We can't even read or write."

Second shepherd: "Oh, don't bother trying to figure it out. That's a waste of time."

First shepherd: "There's probably something in the scriptures about it. Some prophecy that says, 'And an angel shall come to certain poor shepherds pasturing a flock on the hills outside Bethlehem.'"

Third shepherd: "Really? My goodness! To think that we are mentioned in the holy scriptures!"

Second shepherd: "Well, I wouldn't let it go to your head. It could have been anyone. It just happens to be us."

Third shepherd: "Yes, but still …"

First shepherd: "Anyway, we have a job to do. The angel said we had to go to Bethlehem and look for a baby."

Second shepherd: "Wrapped in swaddling clothes and lying in a trough."

Third shepherd: "Why would a baby be lying in a trough? Troughs are for hay."

First shepherd: "Oh, for heaven's sake—are you going to keep asking questions all night? Who *cares* why? We just have to find him. That's what he said. It's our job."

Third shepherd: "Do we leave right now?"

Second shepherd: "It's the middle of the night. No one will be awake."

First shepherd: "We may as well wait till morning."

Third shepherd: "I don't think I can sleep. I'm too excited."

Second shepherd: "I know what you mean. But we should *try* to get some sleep before the others come to relieve us."

First shepherd: "I agree. We should all try. Tomorrow could be a very long day."

2.

When the sun rose, they packed their leather pouches with gifts for the Messiah: two jars of clotted ewe's milk, butter, and a large sheep cheese. Then they set out for Bethlehem. It was an easy walk, and they arrived on the outskirts of the town in less than an hour.

The first stable they saw was a small building made of stones and mortar. A middle-aged woman stood outside it with an armful of straw. When she saw them approach, she hurried into the adjoining house. They looked around, but they could see no one else, so they knocked on the door. A man in soiled work clothes opened it.

"Yes?" he said.

"We're looking for a baby," the first shepherd said.

"A baby?"

"Yes. We're looking for a baby in swaddling clothes, lying in a trough."

"Lying in a trough?"

"Yes."

"Why would a baby be lying in a trough?"

"We don't know, sir."

"Is this a joke?"

"No, sir. Not at all. Is there a baby here?"

"What's this all about? Why are you looking for a baby?"

"Well, to tell you the truth, sir, an angel told us to. The Messiah has just been born! That's the baby we're looking for."

The door slammed shut.

After a while they came to another stable. They entered it warily. There were a dozen cows in it. Two farmers turned to them, leaning on their pitchforks.

"Is there a baby here?" the first shepherd asked in a soft voice.

"What? Couldn't hear you."

"A baby. Do you have a baby here?"

"Out here in the stable? Why would we have a baby here?"

"Well, we're looking for one."

Silence.

"We're looking for a baby lying in a trough."

Silence.

"An angel told us to find a baby in a trough. It's the Messiah. The Messiah has just been born!"

"What are you, crazy? Get out of here!"

"But the Messiah …"

Angry scowls. Raised pitchforks. The shepherds turned and hurried away.

It was like that all morning.

3.

Finally, toward the middle of the afternoon, they came to an inn. It was crowded with pilgrims. They stepped inside, asked for the innkeeper, and waited. Eventually he came, hurrying toward them in a sweat. A baby in a trough? Yes, out in back, in the stable. He pointed them in its direction. "A sweet young couple," he said. "I'm letting them stay here for forty days. She's unclean after the birth, of course. When the time comes, they'll go to Jerusalem and offer a sacrifice at the Temple to purify her, then travel back to their village. Are you friends of theirs? Oh, sorry, I have to go."

The shepherds opened the stable door slowly and tiptoed inside. In one of the stalls stood an ox and next to it a small gray donkey. Across the aisle, a girl sat on a pile of straw with her back propped against the wall. A man stood beside her. Both were looking down at an infant, who was sleeping at their feet in a shallow stone trough.

When the man asked them why they had come, the first shepherd told him about the angel and his message, and the unearthly light that had shone all around them, and the music from the stars, which was wordless but also had words. The man seemed astonished. The girl seemed astonished also, but her expression soon changed. She smiled the tenderest smile they had ever seen.

Then each of the shepherds came forward in turn, kneeled on one knee, and offered them his heartfelt good wishes. They glanced at the baby, then took their gifts from their leather pouches and set them before the man and the girl. As they looked at her, they were filled with pity. There was no fire in the stall and no mother or handmaid to help her. Why hadn't the angel provided a cradle for the baby or brought the girl a feather bed or a blanket or a tub of hot water? And all those spirits singing from the stars, so many hundreds upon hundreds—couldn't a single one of them have come down to earth to lend the poor girl a hand?

But she didn't seem to mind. She thanked them for their gifts and looked them in the eyes, one by one. Each of the shepherds felt profoundly moved.

Later, on their way back to the flock, they told everyone they met what had happened.

Interlude

WELL, THAT WAS THE BEST I COULD DO with the shepherd characters, who are not the sharpest tools in the shed.

The point here is that the birth of the Messiah gladdens the hearts of the humble, the simple-minded, and the illiterate, as well as the hearts of people like you and me. To the mind of Luke, who imagined this part of the story, you can't get any humbler than a shepherd. Besides, in adding shepherds to the mix (Matthew didn't feel the need to; wise men were the figures that appealed to his imagination), Luke was taking advantage of a thousand-year-old tradition that equated shepherds with virtue, from Father Abraham through the young slingshot-savvy, none-too-virtuous David. An ancient Jewish poet had glorified shepherdship even further by making it God's own profession. ("The Lord is my shepherd," etc.)

No one would deny that the opening lines of Psalm

23 are beautiful, but, for me at least, they don't bear a deeper reading. After all, sheep are not the most intelligent of animals, and though I don't mind being compared to a wooly quadruped for a few lines, I don't wish to be herded around in a flock, even to green pastures and still waters, nor do I feel comforted by rods and staffs, however divinely wielded. (A good metaphor works on every level, including the literal.) That's why I prefer thinking in terms of a still, small voice. When that voice says go, I go; when it says stop, I stop. There is no "I" involved, nor are there any words, nor is there any doing. The doing does itself.

A friend of mine bought a house and ten acres of land a hundred miles north of San Francisco. He owned a beloved border collie, and he thought he would please her by giving her an ancestral job, so he bought half a dozen sheep to go along with the property. He also bought a dozen chickens, Rhode Island Reds and Ameraucanas, for their egg value. But Molly showed not the slightest interest in the sheep. She had found her true profession: herding chickens. The sheep, for their part, imprinted on my friend, and he was unanimously elected both sheepdog and shepherd. He told me it would take a dull mind or a very lively one not to be bored with the monotony of watching sheep munch grass for hours on end. It would be more interesting, he said, if there were marauding wolves or jackals to be reckoned with. He had used a slingshot when he was a boy, and he was sure he could re-hone his skills if he ever needed to.

Of course, if we didn't have Luke's shepherds, we wouldn't have the celestial music and the stunning line from the angels' song: "On earth peace, good will toward men," about which I won't—can't—comment. No words could do it justice.

4

Maryam

Every angel is terrifying.

—RAINER MARIA RILKE

1.

The child is sleeping in the stone manger. Yosef has gone out to buy bread and wine. She is pondering things in her heart. She has had much to ponder since the chill spring morning that changed her life.

It is still vivid in her memory, that morning nine months before. It had been raining for an hour—a soft rain that drew itself around the room's silence like a curtain. She was sitting in her chair, a gift from Yosef (he had designed and made it himself). Her eyes had been closed, her hands folded in her lap as she prayed. She had noticed her thoughts settling like the dirt that falls to the bottom of the basin when you wash vegetables.

Her prayer had no words. It was a listening, but not a listening for words. It continued as it had begun, in silence, and silence was its fulfillment. Inside that silence there were no thoughts, no one praying, no one prayed to. She had sunk down into it so deeply that an hour had passed without her being aware of it. When she opened her eyes, it seemed like just a few moments.

Then, suddenly: the archangel. He—or rather it—shimmered at the edges of her awareness, more beautiful than anything she had ever seen. She cried out in wonder, but there was no sound. She could barely feel her body. Was she even breathing? Time had stopped. The whole world had stopped.

The archangel was addressing her. She could tell that it was speaking—if "speaking" was the right word to describe an utterance without words. She had always pictured angels as human in form. But this being was so far beyond any form—beyond anything she could have imagined—that she felt dazed with awe. The being was addressing her with a kindness that she couldn't even begin to fathom. What was it saying? She listened as hard as she could, straining to translate the current of intimacy into terms she could understand.

Then a jolt of dread shot through her. But why should she be afraid of a being who had obviously come to her with the most loving of intentions? She felt an overwhelming urge to pull back into her old life, where everything was so familiar: her room, her friends, the beloved man she was betrothed to, her everyday tasks of cooking, scrubbing, sweeping, doing laundry at the rocky cistern where the women gathered to tread the clothes and exchange the latest gossip, her mother with her old-fashioned manners, her adorable gruff father, the hundred oddities of the village elders that would send her and her friends into fits of uncontrollable giggling. She loved her life. She didn't want it to change.

The Lord is with you.

Ah. That, at least, had formed itself in her listening into human words. Had she grasped the meaning correctly? She felt the light at the circumference of her awareness grow steadier, as though it was signaling that she had understood. Was this the message it had come to deliver: that the Lord was with her? She was very glad, of course, but it was hardly news, and it hardly required an arch-angel. She had known it all her life. She had been taught it by her parents. And indeed all Jewish girls and boys knew that the Lord was with them if they obeyed His commandments. She had lived in that knowledge. Though there had been times when she had been naughty, or angry at her parents, or even (mildly) disobedient, times when she had said something unkind or made fun of someone she disliked, those moments were rare, and she had always been sorry for them and had quickly apologized to anyone she might have offended. Usually she was filled with such delight that an unkind thought would never even arise in her mind. She was grateful for this sweetness of temper, which was a gift from God. She knew how much it meant to her parents—to the whole village, in fact. They loved to see her going about, singing from place to place, with no reason for her joy but the mere fact of being. Many people in Nazareth had told her how much her happiness meant to them.

The Lord had been gracious also in giving her Yosef. She had always felt loved by God, but never so deeply as after Yosef had fallen in love with her. She

had met him only once before her father had told
her that he had asked for her hand in marriage, but
she had liked him immediately, and it took very little
time for her to love him. He was perfect in every way.
Everyone in the village admired him. He was impeccably honest, kind to children and animals, a good son
and brother, charitable to the poor, a hard worker, and
a skilled craftsman whose yokes and plows were prized
throughout Galilee. He was also a modest man, and so
shy with her at first that she'd had to coax the words
out of his mouth. She had known from his eyes that he
loved her, and when he actually said it, it was the most
thrilling thing that had ever happened to anyone since
the beginning of the world. When she was allowed to
be alone with him, it was like standing in the Garden
of Eden, Eve and Adam together, joined in the depths
of their souls, one flesh, in a love that nothing could
ever trouble.

Over the months that followed the betrothal ceremony, Yosef had learned to be less shy with her. He
could look deeply into her eyes now, though sometimes after a few minutes he would blush and turn
away. His modesty touched her, and it amused her
so much that she would sometimes tease him about

it. She herself was not as modest as that. And in her thoughts she was not modest at all. She didn't hesitate to imagine Yosef kissing her on the lips. She would chant the Song of Songs to herself with the beautiful cantillation that her father had taught her and see Yosef's face moving closer to hers. יִשָּׁקֵנִי מִנְּשִׁיקוֹת פִּיהוּ *(Yishakáyni min'shikót píhu), Let him kiss me with the kisses of his mouth.* Before long they would be married, and she would not have to imagine.

The Lord was with her, but that couldn't be the message; there had to be more. The light flickered like a circle of cool flame. All this, she realized, was happening within the space of a single instant—the space of less than an instant. She could see the raindrops outside her window, which had been falling from the sky, hundreds of them, suspended now in midair. All the everyday sounds of the village—the hammering, the barking, the braying, the mothers calling after their children—had stopped. It was miraculous, but it also seemed matter-of-fact, as though she were in a dream. She brought her attention back to the angel's brightness, eloquent in its own unfathomable way and yet so difficult for her human mind to translate. The angel was trying to calm her. It meant for her not to be afraid. She could feel her heart pounding. She *was* afraid. But of what?

2.

A brief pause now. I want to consider the idea of the angel, which has been sentimentalized beyond recognition by contemporary Christian and New Age teachers alike.

In my story, angels are reflections of human consciousness; thus, the forms they take vary in accordance with the spiritual maturity of the observer. The tall, fiery-haired, unblinking angel who appears to the shepherds exists at the limit of what they can endure. In chapter five, Yosef's dream angel will be adorned with the golden hair, Renaissance robes, and multicolor wings of Fra Angelico, but he is dangerous enough to have fierce green animal-eyes. Maryam's angel, on the other hand, given the purity of her heart, is a being of a different order. Though the traditional Gabriel is a male, I have tried to describe it (not "him") in nonphysical terms, and an image of light was the best I could come up with. But since I was bound by the details of the Annunciation story, the light had to be able to speak in intelligible human terms.

The person who thought most meticulously about this imaginary being was the Catholic theologian Thomas Aquinas. According to him, the angel is pure intelligence, freed of any limits imposed by a union with matter. Since the angel has no body, it is neither "he" nor "she"; since it has no sexual incompleteness to overcome, it is whole in a way that a human either-male-or-female can never be. Not only is it not divided into sexes; it is not divided at all; it is whole in all possible ways. It is the ideal intellect, the clear thinker's clearest thinker, the created being who most completely understands the truth. There is nothing more sublime in the whole universe, according to Aquinas, and nothing we can more appropriately aspire to: "The ultimate human felicity is found in the operation of the intellect, since no desire carries us to such heights as the desire to understand the truth. Indeed, all our desires for pleasure or for other things can be satisfied, but the desire to understand does not rest until it reaches God."

As opposed to the human intellect, the angel has no need to observe the world, no need to acquire knowledge from physical things. It is able to dispense with the clumsy mechanism of logic, since it has direct understanding of the way things are. It knows the truth intuitively, entirely, and within itself. And in the act of intuiting one truth, it instantaneously grasps all the manifold consequences of that truth. The eureka moment—Newton's apple or Kekulé's snakes—the breath-stopping inspiration, the dazzle of insight that sees heaven in a wild flower: these are the normal modes of its intelligence. Nor does it communicate by a means so gross as speech; its communication is immediate and complete; for it, empathy and telepathy are synonymous. Its mind is to the human mind what dancing is to slogging through mud.

If you pursue this idea to its limit, you'll find yourself imagining an inconceivably joyful society of disembodied beings more numerous than the stars, hierarchically ranked by the quality of their intelligence, all participating in the beatific vision to the fullness of their vast and vaster capacities. Billions upon billions of these lovely, love-informed minds direct the planets and guide the affairs of the universe, all in many-layered harmony with one another, all in supernal bliss.

Maryam is facing one of the highest-ranking angels—an archangel in fact. It's a consciousness that from the beginning of their encounter constitutes a challenge, even to a human mind as pure as hers. And in fact, the angel is the *embodiment* of challenge, according to the great twentieth-century poet Rainer Maria Rilke; it "with tilted brow dismisses / anything that circumscribes or binds." His poem "The Angel" ends with an image of life-transforming and ego-shattering confrontation. If you were to give yourself over to this angel, Rilke tells us, someday, some night, the angel's light hands

> would come more fiercely to interrogate you,
> and rush to seize you blazing like a star,
> and bend you, as if trying to create you,
> and break you open, out of who you are.

The encounter with Maryam is about to intensify. We're about to see why every angel, even the kindest, is terrifying.

3.

You will conceive.

Ah, so that was the message! She could understand the wordless communication more easily now.

The angel was deep inside her, or was she inside the angel? It was as though she were *hearing* the light—though "light" was the wrong word, since the radiance was not something that her eyes, or any of her senses, could perceive. But the angel had come to tell her that she would have a son. She was sure of it now.

The news filled her with joy. She hadn't doubted her ability to conceive, but to have it confirmed in this way was thrilling. How happy Yosef would be! They had never talked about having children, but there had been no need to, since God had commanded them, as He had commanded every Jewish couple, to be fruitful and multiply. Did the angel mean that she would become pregnant the very first time she and Yosef came together? Wouldn't that be perfect! They had been betrothed for almost a year now and were legally bound to each other, exactly as if they were married. The wedding would take place in less than a month, and then the wedding contract would be signed, and he would bring her to his house, and the child would be born in the month of Sh'vat. But if she didn't conceive the first time, that would be perfect too. It would happen soon, though. This must be what the angel had come to tell her.

But why should an angel come to tell her anything?

It was very strange. It made her uneasy. She was not an old woman like the matriarch Sarah, who needed a miracle before she could conceive, and as far as she knew she wasn't barren like Rebecca or Rachel. She was just an ordinary girl, about to be married. Why had she been favored in this way? She had never prayed for a child. She had never prayed for anything—or if for something, only for God's grace, which she knew she already had, if "had" was the right word. Was there something special about the baby? Was that why the angel had come? Was it just to announce that she would be giving birth to a son rather than a daughter?

You will name him Yeshua.

She smiled. It was a good name, Yeshua. It was short for Yehoshua: "The Lord Is Salvation," which was certainly true. Nothing could be truer.

He will be great.

She tried to take this in. Great? Is that what the angel had said? But *goodness* was what she wanted for the child. What was greatness, anyway but power and wealth? She had never known any of the great. None of them would have deigned to visit a nondescript village like Nazareth, with its dirt lanes and six hundred artisans and farmers. She wanted the boy to be as good a man as his father, a happy child, a happy man, who loved God, loved his neighbor, and was fulfilled in his work and family. Wasn't that what every mother wanted for her son? God forbid that he should become one of the high-and-mighty.

But she mustn't leap to conclusions. Perhaps by "great" the angel meant something else. She realized that he—it—was being extremely patient with her. For her sake it had temporarily deleted time, so that, like the raindrops, she was suspended in the air of her own mind. Now she had all the time in the world to contemplate the angel's statements as they became intelligible. At first, each one threatened to over-whelm her. But the fear ebbed as she understood or tried to understand. Greatness: might that not refer to something other than the arrogant rich, whom she had heard about from her father and had glimpsed on her few visits to Sepphoris, with their slaves and fine linen and silks and jewels and tinkling feet? If the child grew up to achieve greatness, as the angel was saying, might it not be as a scholar, a rabbi? He might grow up to be a wise man, filled with the un-derstanding of God's ways and able to comfort his people. That would be something to warm any Jew-ish mother's heart.

He will be called the son of the Most High.

She felt her breath catch. "Son of God" meant "king." Surely the message had nothing to do with kingship. No, that was not the angel's meaning, surely. It must be that the child would grow up to be one of the righteous. "All who are led by the spirit of God are sons of God," she had heard a visiting rabbi say in the village synagogue; they are sons of God because they resemble their Father in heaven, manifesting His kindness and generosity in their love for His commandments. Because they are free men, the rabbi had said, God has freely adopted them and is as proud of them as a human father is of his beloved sons. And surely, if anyone ever was a son of God, Yosef was. So Yeshua would be a son of God too. This must be the good news the angel had brought her.

But perhaps the phrase had the other meaning, the one about kingship. She was her father's daughter, after all, the daughter of a priest, and many times she had heard her father ranting against kings. Everyone knew the psalm in which God says to King David, "You are my son; today I have begotten you." So every king of Israel, the rabbis said, was the son of God—the unrighteous kings as well as the righteous, the unwise as well as the wise. But then the meaning was merely a formality, wasn't it? It was just a manner of speaking and had nothing to do with the truth. If a wicked king was nonetheless a "son of God," what value did that phrase have? How could it be honest? And what mother would want her son to be a king if he acted in opposition to God's law, betraying his mission and bringing misery on his people?

Besides, how could her child be next in line for the throne? Herod was the king—an Edomite, not even a Jew! And if, by some miracle, God should cause a revolution and return the kingdom to his own people, how could the son of a village craftsman be chosen to rule over it? There had been twenty or more generations since the Babylonian captivity, and of the thousands or tens of thousands of people descended from David, how could it be that Yosef's branch of the family should have precedence over them all? It was the most unlikely of possibilities.

The Lord God will give him the throne of his forefather David.

Ah, so it *was* that second meaning! How could it possibly be? But how could an angel be wrong? She felt a twinge of disappointment. She had grown up in a priestly family with a strong prejudice against kings—not a prejudice but a clearly reasoned and firmly held opinion. Her father was passionate, even vehement, about it. She could remember many discussions around the dinner table when one or several of the village elders had come to dine with him and the subject of kings had arisen and her father had ended up shouting and pounding on the table. (She and her mother served them from the kitchen, but they were allowed to come in and listen to the conversation.)

It was not just Herod whom he would inveigh against—Herod, who had committed every kind of atrocity, murdering his own wife and children, crucifying thousands of righteous men, grinding down the poor with a heavy burden of taxes and spending the money on buildings that reeked of excess and pride: theaters and palaces and the new Temple, which, in her father's eyes, was for all time and eternity polluted by the crimes of its builder. Not only Herod but *every* king was an abomination, her father would shout, even the greatest—David, who was a rank adulterer, a murderer as well, and Solomon, a man so lascivious that even seven hundred wives and three hundred concubines couldn't satisfy his lust. (At this point, red in the face, he would send her out of the room.)

Her father would also call on the prophet Samuel as witness. Samuel too was a priest, and he had warned the people about kings, though the people hadn't listened. A king will take your children, Samuel had said. Your sons will serve in his army and your daughters in his palace. A king will give power to his favorites; he will confiscate your land, tax you to pay for his extravagances, and act to ensure his own good, not yours. And a day will come when you will bitterly regret that you ever wanted a king to be placed above you.

She tried to imagine her child growing up to be king of Israel, but it seemed unreal; she could see only vague images of golden cups and marble columns. It must be a good thing, though, if it was what God wanted. Her father, bless his heart, was wrong then; though it had never happened before, it must really be possible for a king to be a righteous man. If her son was to become the king of Galilee—or of Galilee, Samaria, and Judea combined—perhaps he would change everything. Certainly he would change everything. He would scatter the great in their arrogance, pull down the mighty from their seats and exalt those who are humble, fill the hungry with good things and send the rich away empty. A king can do these things. He can confiscate some of the wealth of the nobles and the merchants and use it to help those who are truly in need. God had always said, through His prophets, that the duty of the righteous was to feed the poor and to succor the widow and orphan. How wonderful if her son could make that happen!

And he will reign over the people of Israel forever.

Forever? Did that mean that he would become the long-awaited one, the Messiah? Could that really be? No one had ever prophesied that the Messiah would never die. They had said that he would come and drive out the foreign armies, and the land would be free, and a thousand years of peace would follow. Her father had told her the prophecies many times, ever since she was a little girl. He had sat at her bedside or taken her onto his lap after morning prayers, and in the gentlest, sweetest tones he had told her what the Lord had promised through the mouths of Isaiah and the other prophets. She had listened to him entranced, marveling as she watched the harsh lines on his face relax.

When she had closed her eyes, she could see the future right in front of her: how the nations would beat their swords into plowshares and their spears into pruning hooks and war would vanish from the earth. Abiding peace—that was the sign. That was how people would know that the Messiah had finally come. There would be no more wickedness; everyone would be kind to everyone else, and everyone would learn God's ways and walk in His paths, and out of Zion the law would go forth and the word of the Lord from Jerusalem. If all this was truly about to happen, what a joy it would be for her father and for all Israel, and for everyone on earth! And really, did it matter if it was her child who was the Messiah or if it was someone else's child? What mattered was that he should be born, so that the whole world might be transformed, the crooked be made straight and the rough places plain, and the glory of the Lord be revealed, and all people on earth—Jews and Gentiles alike—see it together.

No wonder the angel had come! It was all going to happen, the dream that her father had been dreaming all his life—it was all going to come true now! There would be no more violence or cruelty; people would love their neighbors and care for them as if for their own family; selfishness would vanish and be a thing of the ancient, benighted past. There would be no distinction between rich or poor: all people would be provided for, all would be sons and daughters of the Most High, blessing life and rejoicing in His infinite love. Death would eventually come, of course, as it must, to all mortal beings, but people would die not in fear, they would die like Abraham and Job, old and satisfied and full of days. She could barely contain her emotion. She felt like David's cup, running over with joy.

The Holy Spirit will come upon you …

What? Another jolt of dread shot through her body.

… and the power of the Most High will overshadow you.

Overpowered, overshadowed by the Holy Spirit? Terror was only a part of what she felt now. She tried to sort out the emotions. Disgust, confusion, even (could it be?) a flash of anger. She had heard from her father about the gods of the Romans, stories that were filthy from beginning to end, he would say, spitting on the ground three times in passionate contempt. The filthiest of the stories were about Jupiter, their sky god, who would descend to earth and rape young women, disguising himself as a bull or a swan or even, in a refinement of cruelty, as a woman's beloved husband, filling them with his seed so that they would give birth to what the Gentiles called heroes. Was the angel saying now that God would descend upon her in this way, impregnating her as Jupiter impregnated those poor unwilling girls? Did God have a body, then? Had He chosen her as His concubine, God forbid? That couldn't possibly be true. But what else could this "overshadowing" mean? She blushed at the very thought of it.

Or would God simply, without touching her, plant a male seed in her womb? Or would there be no seed at all? Would He somehow miraculously quicken one of her eggs without any male involved? Being a village girl, she knew that chicken's eggs couldn't harbor life without being fertilized first, and she had seen cows covered by bulls and stray dogs mating in the street. It was no different for humans. Was she to be made an exception then, a freak? And how, after all, would the Holy Spirit "come upon" her? It frightened her to think of it: some massive force pressing down on her body or some huge winged thing swooping down on her from out of the sun and engulfing her in its shadow.

How could she fathom any of this? And did she even have a choice? Could she say no? Would the Almighty, the maker of heaven and earth, let her even open her mouth to utter a stifled cry? She felt her body shudder. This was not what she wanted. But how could it be wrong if it had been announced to her by a being so surpassingly beautiful and kind? She struggled with this contradiction as uneasily as though she were tossing in her sleep. The message *had* to be something beautiful, but she couldn't see how.

And there was something else. What about Yosef? It was *his* child that she wanted to bear. Did the angel mean that Yosef was not righteous enough to be the father of the Messiah? But what human could be any more righteous than that beautiful man, a man without sin, she was sure, like the prophets Noah and Job. Wouldn't this impregnation make a mockery of her marriage? People get married, after all, because they love each other and want to become intimate in every way. They leave their fathers and mothers, holy scripture says, and cleave to each other's bodies and become one flesh in the child that they beget. Having children is a commandment for married people. Why then was she being called upon to bypass Yosef with her firstborn son? As his wife, she could imagine no greater honor than to be the vessel for his seed. What was more just than that his goodness be passed on to their child? It seemed unfair to have a child without him, if such a thing was possible—and it must be possible, since the angel said it was. But wouldn't that be a kind of adultery, God forbid, even if it was with the Holy Spirit? She had given herself to Yosef with all her heart, and she had never felt the slightest conflict between her love for him and her love for God. It was the same love. He was God's gift to her. So how could she be asked to turn her back on him at the very point of union between husband and wife?

She was appalled to think of how he would react to the news: "Yosef, I am with child." Could she look him in the eyes and say that? It would break his heart. He wouldn't believe her, of course, when she told him what had happened. As a reasonable person, he wouldn't be *able* to believe her. No one would. And then what? Since he was a good man, his only choice would be to put her aside. But even with a private divorce, she would be shamed in the sight of everyone, as a depraved woman, an adulteress. The whole village would treat her with contempt; she would be despised and rejected by them all. Her father would certainly disown her. And how would she care for the baby? Who would be there to help her? Not her mother. Not anyone.

The worst of it was that she would lose Yosef's love. Nothing she could say would be able to heal his wound. And later on, there would be the anguish of hearing that he had married another woman. How could she bear that? She knew that God, in His infinite wisdom, would ask nothing of her that she was not capable of doing. But this—was this truly what He was asking of her now? She wanted to do His will. But she prayed to Him that He might change His mind. She prayed that He might require something else of her—anything else.

4.

Another brief pause for some comments. When most people think of the Annunciation story, they picture Mary as an obedient schoolgirl, stereotypically passive and accommodating. Though they may imagine her dressed in sumptuous blue and red robes (Botticelli) or in a more modest blue-and-white outfit (Fra Angelico), she might as well be wearing a white shirt, tie, above-the-knee plaid skirt, and long socks, so schoolgirlish is the traditional concept of her.

GABRIEL: "You will conceive," etc.

MARY: "But how can I be pregnant? I've never had sex with a man."

GABRIEL: "The Holy Spirit will come upon you," etc.

MARY: "Oh. Okay."

But surrender is never easy. There are two powerful examples of this in the Hebrew Bible. In the Book of Genesis, Jacob wrestles with a so-called angel, which turns out to be God. The writer states simply that "a [supernatural] being wrestled with him until dawn." We tend to imagine Jacob's struggle at the ford of the Jabbok as though it were one of our professional wrestling or boxing matches, which last for less than an hour. But Jacob was wrestling for eight or nine hours, from nightfall until daybreak. Can you imagine doing that? Wrestling with a strong human, when it's a matter of life and death, would be exertion enough, during what would seem like an interminable period. But wrestling with a supernatural being? All night long? This story is a parable about an inner spiritual struggle. I like to think of it as a struggle with Jacob's idea of God. Victory over his image of God is surrender to the God beyond all images. It's one of the clearest parables we have.

The second example comes from the Book of Isaiah. In about 740 BCE, the prophet had a vision: he saw God sitting on a high throne in the Temple, surrounded by a multitude of six-winged seraphim—a high order of angels characterized by their burning love for God—who were calling "Holy, holy, holy is the Lord Almighty; the whole earth is filled with His glory!" But rather than being exalted by this vision, Isaiah felt crushed. "Woe is me!" he cried out. "I am ruined" (the Hebrew verb can also mean "I am silenced" or "I am struck dumb"), "for I am a man of unclean lips."

What does "unclean lips" mean? Isaiah might have been remembering actual sins (in other words, serious mistakes) he had committed with his mouth, words he had spoken in anger or disrespect. But I think he was also referring to something more basic: his inability to say anything that would be even remotely worthy of God. He had, after all, just heard the ecstatic fiery music of the seraphim, translated, in human language, into the verse I quoted above, which might have been written by William Blake. He was struck dumb by that music. He realized that, in contrast to the seraphim, there was nothing truthful, nothing even valid that he could say about God, and yet, as a messenger of God, it was his duty to speak. In addition, he might have remembered the verse from Exodus that said, "No human may see me and live." So he owed God a death—not later but now.

What happens next is, for me, unutterably moving:

Then one of the seraphim picked up a pair of tongs and took a burning coal from the altar,

and he flew down to me and pressed it to my
mouth and said, "Now that this has touched
your lips, your sin has been taken away." Then
I heard the voice of the Lord saying, "Whom
shall I send, and who will go for us?" And I
said, "Here I am. Send me."

Can you enter into this image as well? The huge
six-winged seraph approaches with tongs holding a
white-hot coal and, without your conscious permission, presses the coal to your lips. For one second? Five
minutes? An hour? You feel an almost unbearable
pain. You smell your flesh burning. Your legs tremble
so violently that they can barely keep you standing.
This is happening at one of the most intimate places
on your body, the place that suckled at your mother's
breast, that takes in food, that kisses your beloved. And
you die into the pain. You brace yourself against it at
first; then you endure it; then you invite it, because you
know that it's a necessary part of your transformation
and that without it you'll remain a person of unclean
lips. You realize that it's your only chance to become
what you long to be: an unalloyed servant of the truth,
a transparent vehicle for the voice that will say, in human language, what is ultimately unsayable.

And after the coal has done its job and your ego has been burned to extinction, you say, "Here I am." In Hebrew this is one word: הִנֵּנִי, *hinéyni*, with no separate "here" or "I" or "am" in it. It's a gesture not of obedience but of presence. I imagine Isaiah, like Abraham before him, standing with his arms spread, in complete readiness for whatever the still, small voice might command.

Maryam too will come to this place inside her. She will struggle and die and surrender into the "Here I am."

5.

Therefore the child to be born will be holy.

She wanted that, of course. But why had the angel said *therefore*? Did it mean that only a child without a human father could be holy? How could that be? Wasn't the very act of love between a husband and wife the essence of holiness, as she had been taught? What about the great sages and prophets? What about Abraham, Isaac, and Jacob? Weren't they holy? But they all had human fathers. And Abraham's father had been an idolater!

The light glowed in and out—more intense, then less—a pulse of radiance. She felt soothed. She thought she understood what the angel was saying. Her questions would not be answered; they didn't need to be answered. And she did have a choice. She could say no. She could return to her old life. The decision was hers.

But how could she say no to the birth of the Messiah, which would bring peace to all Israel and all the world, however much grief it might cause her personally? She would have to give up everything she held dear: Yosef, her parents and grandparents, her friends. As soon as they knew she was pregnant, her life with them would be over. Even if they could somehow, someday, forgive her (for what she hadn't done), she would always be known as the woman who had committed adultery—a shame and disgrace never to be forgotten.

Why was *she* the one who had been chosen for this? She was just an ordinary girl, no prettier, smarter, or more virtuous than a hundred other girls in a hundred villages throughout the land. Why couldn't God choose one of *them*? Why choose a virgin and complicate matters? There was no reason to. "Behold, the young woman shall conceive and bear a son," Isaiah had prophesied, so it could be a young wife as well as an unmarried girl. If it had to be her, why not wait for her to marry Yosef and have the child with him, a legitimate son of the house of David? The Messiah could be born then, and she would be left with the life that was so dear to her. Furthermore, if the son wasn't Yosef's, if it was only hers, how could he be king, since she descended from the tribe of Levi, and it was only through a human father that the child could descend from the tribe of Judah, David's tribe?

She felt an amused or a compassionate "no" coming from the angel—a flicker in the radiance, which might have been a smile if there had been a face. No, it was saying, *she* was the chosen one. No other woman was possible. And it had to be done without a father. It was not for her to bargain with the Almighty or to change the terms of the request.

Panic in her heart. If she said no, the Messiah would not be born. Not ever? Was that what the angel meant? But if she was the chosen one, surely she would be allowed to think about her decision, to discuss it with Yosef. He was so much wiser than she was. He would be able to discern what was right and what was wrong, as he always did, and make the correct choice, which would naturally be hers as well. And furthermore, since the decision would affect him as much as it would affect her, he was surely entitled to have a share in it, wasn't he?

Another flicker of amusement or (could it be?) of compassion—from the angel, as though it saw something that was hidden from her. No, she would not be able to consult with Yosef. She would have to decide in this instant, though since the instant had been severed from past and future, it could last for as long as she wished. She would have to do it alone. There was no one in heaven or on earth who could help her.

She wanted to say yes to the angel, but she realized that she had to do it with all her heart. She had to surrender herself completely to God's will, not just make a mere dutiful submission. And to do that, she needed to contemplate what her yes would entail, with all its consequences.

What would it mean? She would certainly not be able to stay in Nazareth. She would have to go to Sepphoris, where no one knew her. Capernaum was twenty miles away—too far for her to reach on foot in a weakened condition. After the birth, as soon as she could—or even before the birth, before her belly became too large—she would walk the four miles to Sepphoris. People might be kind to her. Perhaps some traveler on the road would let her ride in his cart. When she got there, she would make her way to some rich man's house and plead to work in his kitchen. She was a hard worker, she would say, and she would make a good scullery maid, though she needed to have the baby with her. She would go to a dozen, a hundred houses if need be. Someone, surely, would take pity on her.

And if no one did, she would sit in the streets and beg. She didn't think that she had much pride, but whatever pride was in her she would surrender in order to keep herself and the baby alive. Her people had never been destitute; they had always been able to feed their family and keep a humble roof over their heads. They considered themselves fortunate, and they spoke of the poor with compassion, donating a part of their meager earnings to support those who had nothing. She had never imagined that she herself, the daughter of a respectable priestly family, would be reduced to beggary. But she could take this on too.

She also realized that she would have to lie. She would not lie to Yosef or to her parents. But when she got to Sepphoris, she would be obliged to. She could see no other way. When people asked her who the child's father was, how could she say it was the Holy Spirit?

"Oh no, sir, the child has no father. God is his father. I am a virgin. I have never slept with a man." People would think she was out of her mind. They would think that a demon had taken possession of her, and they would bind her with chains and take the baby away. She could never let that happen. So she would have to say that she had been unchaste—or better—that she had been raped. It would break her heart to lie. But it was too dangerous not to. This also she could take on.

What comforted her most when she tried to imagine the future was the knowledge that the child would survive, whatever happened to her. God would protect him and preserve him, if not forever, then at least until peace was established over all the earth. She herself might starve. She accepted that possibility. She knew she was not important. But the baby was. He would lead a long and happy life. It gave her great joy to know this.

She thought of the gold ring that she would never be able to wear again, which Yosef had put on her finger during the betrothal ceremony, saying, הֲרֵי אַתְּ מְקֻדֶּשֶׁת לִי *(Haréi át mekudéshet lí)*, *"Behold, you are made holy to me with this ring, according to the law of Moses and Israel."* She had daydreamed about the ring. It was like their love, she had thought: perfect, precious, with no beginning or end. She knew that she was as holy to him as he was to her and that her love for him would never end. But his love for her—it would be over as soon as she told him. How could a righteous man like Yosef love a depraved woman? She had thought that their souls were bound together. She had considered herself faithful for all time, like Ruth the Moabite. "Whither thou goest, I will go." Who could possibly have imagined that she would have to go away from the man she loved more than life itself?

She had been taught that the primal commandment was to love God with all her heart. It had been easy for her to do that, since she had been blessed with indulgent parents and a comfortable life. Gratitude was not an emotion she had ever needed to summon up. It pervaded her world like the air she breathed. She would slip in and out of prayer all day long. It was as effortless as moving from the kitchen to the bedroom. Prayer, for her, was not an asking; it was a stillness, a deepening, a recognition that the world was very good and that everything and everyone in it was taken care of forever. God loved her, her parents loved her, her husband-to-be loved her. Had any girl ever been graced with such abundance?

And now, at this crucial moment, the first difficult moment of her life, what did it mean to love God with all her heart? It had to mean surrendering herself to His will so completely that it became her own will: not merely accepting reality but loving it. So His choice had to be her choice, completely. Love could mean nothing else. She couldn't say no to anything God asked of her. And she couldn't respond with a grudging or a half-hearted or a sorrowful yes, a yes with the slightest reservation. Her yes would have to be total. It would have to be given with the joy of total assent, as in the verse from Isaiah where the lame man leaps like a deer and the mute cries out with songs of praise.

Inevitably she would have to choose between God and Yosef—that is, between God and herself. The choice was obvious. On the one side was a happy life; on the other was the blessedness of all mankind. How could she hold back? What did it matter, ultimately, if one insignificant girl from an insignificant village had her heart broken and broke the heart of the person she loved most? Sooner or later their grief would pass, as all things pass. One day, when her son grew up and established God's kingdom, she might be the only suffering human left on the whole earth. What a comfort it would be then to know that everyone else was happy, however wretched she was—to know that her son was doing what he had come for, feeding the hungry, giving strength to the weak, relieving the widow and orphan, and that he was forever safe in God's care. And even if she was not allowed to keep the memory of this encounter with the angel, even if it should all be erased from her mind as soon as it was over, she would still be comforted when the kingdom came, knowing nothing about her share in its coming.

She felt like the poorest of the poor, stripped of everything she had thought of as her possession: home, family, marriage. Nothing of it was left. It had all been lost in the decision she had made, though until now she hadn't known she had made it. She was surprised to discover that she felt no bitterness, despite the devastation in her heart. There was nothing now between her and God—no reasons, no expectations. *I am the handmaid of the Lord*, she thought. *My soul glorifies Him, and my spirit rejoices in Him, for He has looked on me with favor despite my humble condition. I am at His service, now and always. Let Him use me as He sees fit.*

She could hear a kind of music in the background of her mind. Was that music the words of her thoughts as they arose, or was it the element they arose into?

She couldn't tell if the angel was still there. If not, it had left an afterglow behind it.

She was with child.

Interlude

EXCEPT FOR ITS FIRST PARAGRAPH, this chapter doesn't describe a Christmas scene at all. It focuses on the Annunciation story, because that's where the drama lies. But the Annunciation is enfolded within the Nativity story, as part of Maryam's awareness. The infant Yeshua is her yes become visible, her word become flesh.

As she sits in the chilly barn, gazing at the child asleep in the manger, the thought that he is the Messiah keeps fading from her mind. Her wonder is more primal than any thought could be. Whatever else the child is, he is totally vulnerable, totally dependent on her and Yosef. And though he has, in the words of Isaiah, been born to us all, in this moment he has been born to her alone, and there is no way to contain her joy.

5

Yosef

After the final no there comes a yes
And on that yes the future world depends.

—WALLACE STEVENS

1.

SHE CAME TO HIS WORKSHOP at the end of the day as his men were packing up the tools and leaving. There was an anxious expression on her dear face. She said that she wanted to speak with him out in the lane.

When she told him, he didn't understand. *Angel. Holy Spirit. With child.* He asked her to say it again. But he could make no sense of it. Had she lost her mind? He had never had an unhappy moment with her before, and now, in his confusion, rather than burst into … what—anger? tears?—he turned from her without a word, walked back in, and shut the door.

He felt stunned. Waves of grief surged through his body. He thought that if he picked up an ax or a hammer, he would smash the whole shop—the whole village—to pieces.

Why had she betrayed him? Who was the man? How could she have suddenly turned into that kind of woman: an adulteress, a whore? She hadn't even had the decency to beg for his forgiveness.

He paced back and forth. The whole workshop disgusted him. The rows of tools on the wall, his faithful servants—axes, saws, drills, vices, lathes, hammers, chisels—now seemed fit only to smash and tear. He dared not pick one up.

How could she have done it? How could she have betrayed him? She was like the woman in Proverbs: "This is the way of the adulteress—she eats, then she wipes her mouth and says, 'I have done nothing wrong.'" She was as brazen as that. His beloved Maryam: an adulteress, a whore. It made him sick at heart. "I have seen you commit adultery," the prophet Jeremiah had said, "moaning with lust; I have seen you spread your legs upon every high hill and under every green tree." No, God help him, not there, he must not go there. He gave his mind a harsh tug on the reins. He would not permit it to do that. If he let himself imagine her mating with that faceless man, he would be lost.

He stopped pacing and dried his eyes with his sleeve. He had to master himself. This couldn't be the way. There was no peace in it, only desolation and madness.

He sat down on a chair and closed his eyes. Perhaps he could pray, if prayer was possible among all the thoughts swirling through his mind.

יהוה רֹעִי לֹא אֶחְסָר *(Adonái ro'í, ló eḥsár)*, he chanted. *The Lord is my shepherd; I shall not want*, there is nothing I lack, there is nothing I need that I do not have. He wanted this to ring true for him, but it didn't. He lacked everything now; everything dear to him was gone. He prayed that God would undo what had happened, though he knew that this thought too led to madness. *Almighty God*, he prayed, *blot out what has happened. Remove it from the rolls of the past and return everything to what it was when my cup ran over with happiness. Take this agony from me. Restore my soul. Lead me in the paths of righteousness for Thy name's sake.*

But what would the paths of righteousness look like now? Could he cut Maryam out of his memory, out of his heart, and cauterize the wound with burning iron? Or was he to see her sin as punishment for some dark unwitting sin of his own? He could find no peace in this, no way forward.

לֹא אִירָא רָע כִּי אַתָּה עִמָּדִי (Ló irá rá, kí attá immadí), I will fear no evil, for Thou art with me.

Even as he chanted these words, he realized that for him they were a lie. He *did* fear evil. It had just happened—the greatest of evils—and he feared it would happen again. He feared he would go insane. He feared he would run out of the workshop screaming and drown the whole village in his humiliation and grief, and run to her house, and grab her by the shoulders, and slap her or shake her until she answered a question he didn't even know how to ask. Where was the Lord now? Not here, not amid this swirling chaos. But if the Lord was not with him, it was his own fault. He knew that. God had not left him; he had left God. It could be no other way. He wanted to dwell in the house of the Lord forever, but here he was, naked and shivering in the wilderness, lost, no longer even knowing where the Lord's house was, or how to find his way back to it, or how to know that it even existed.

It frightened him to be so angry. But no, it wasn't his anger that frightened him; it was Maryam's depravity. She hadn't even said that she was sorry or asked for his forgiveness. How could a virtuous young woman fall into wickedness just like that? How could she spread her legs and … No. Do *not.* Do not go there. *The Lord is my shepherd. The Lord is my shepherd.*

None of it made sense. Was he going mad? Had he been out of his mind when he fell in love with her? Yet her parents were respectable people, and she had a good reputation—*more* than good. People loved her; they delighted in her. He had always trusted his own judgment, and the first time he saw her he had known—or was that too a delusion?—that the young woman was extraordinary. It was not her beauty that had struck him. He had never taken much notice of women. He honored his mother, of course, and he was an affectionate brother to his two sisters. But he considered women to be distractions from his life of service to God—creatures too frivolous to be worth much of his attention. It was different with Maryam. What had struck him about her was not her beauty but the radiance of her eyes. She was a modest girl, and in company she kept her glance mostly directed at the floor. But when they were introduced, she had suddenly looked up at him with those brilliant blue eyes, and he had felt penetrated through and through, as though the sun had blazed into his soul. Nothing of the sort had ever happened to him before, and nothing in his life had been the same afterward. He knew immediately that she would be his wife and the mother of his children. She was the אֵשֶׁת חַיִל *(éshet ḥáyil),* the excellent woman of Proverbs, whose value was far greater than rubies.

He had felt this in the first instant of seeing her, and everything that followed seemed to bear out his intuition. After the betrothal ceremony he was allowed to meet her often. It was usually in the company of her mother, but sometimes alone, and the more he knew of her, the more in love he was. Not only in love: in awe. She was graced with a quality he had been striving for all his life, ever since he had realized what his purpose, what the purpose of every Jew, was: to love God with all his heart and to fulfill His commandments as impeccably and with as much joy as he could summon. Maryam didn't need to summon joy; it was always with her. Happiness seemed to be always flowing out of her heart and filling her eyes with its luster. It was a quality he called blessedness. She seemed to be filled with a knowledge of God that he himself would have given almost anything in the world to attain. When she spoke of God, it was not of some august being who dwelled in the highest heavens, at an infinite remove from earth; it was of a presence nearer than breath, than heartbeat. She seemed to have been spared the ordinary human problems that even the righteous must face. She had been left with nothing but gratitude and laughter.

Sometimes, when he was alone with her, she would go into a state of rapture. She would close her eyes and sit there with an indescribably blissful smile on her face. Tears streamed down her cheeks. Her mouth dropped open, and occasionally a trickle of saliva ran down her chin and fell onto the front of her robe. These periods of rapture would last from ten minutes to half an hour, and after the first one he learned to recognize the signs. He would sit and watch her in awe. From time to time he would get up, walk over, and with his handkerchief dry her eyes or wipe the saliva from her chin, then sit back down and keep watching. He had never heard or read of anything like it. It was as though God's love were streaming into her soul the way light rushes into a transparent object. He never asked her to describe what she experienced during these states; he felt he had no right to. Afterward, she would open her eyes, smile, and carry on the conversation as though nothing had happened.

He had been very grateful that he didn't envy her this blessedness. It was not that he wouldn't have wanted it for himself as well. But it was clear that this was *her* gift; it was not meant for him—not yet at least. It would have been as senseless to envy it as to be unhappy because he was not as wise as Solomon or as eloquent as David. He knew that God, in His infinite generosity, gave to every creature just as much as that creature's capacity could hold. In that sense, he thought, generosity was another name for justice. And truly, he wanted no more for himself than what he already had. He was well aware that if he had desired a joy like hers, he would not have been in harmony with Him whose love had assigned him to a lower station. So he didn't envy the purity of her soul, nor did he wish for anything greater than his own mediocrity.

He got up from his chair, walked to the front of the workshop, and opened the door. There was no one in the lane but a stray dog, a poor emaciated creature that loped along with its muzzle to the ground. The sun was beginning to dip toward the horizon, streaking the sky with red. The air was cool. He could smell the rain coming. He closed the door, walked back to his chair, and sat down again.

As he prayed—or attempted to pray, in the midst

of his confusion and sorrow—he realized that the fissure between past and present ran through everything in his mind. Had he been deluded about Maryam from the beginning? No. He was sure that what he had seen in her was real—the realest of the real. And yet she was pregnant. How could that be? Had he dreamed it? It was as though he were looking at two different women with his two eyes: one eye saw the blessed girl he had fallen in love with, the other the faithless woman, the whore. There was no depth vision; he couldn't bring the two images together. Was it even possible for someone who knew God's love as intimately as she did to become depraved? How could that be? It made no sense. But that was what had happened, according to her own words.

And now he was called upon to act as a righteous man, to put his bitterness aside and respond to her sin in a way that would be impeccably fair-minded. He had never thought much about sin. It was something that other people committed. He could barely comprehend it. Even if he made a great effort, he could only begin to imagine himself in the position of someone who cheated or stole or dishonored his parents or desecrated the Sabbath. These things could happen only when people didn't understand the First Commandment: not to put other gods before the Unnamable One. The idol of selfhood was powerful and seductive, and if you separated yourself from God by worshiping it, you walked down a path that led to almost irreparable harm, for yourself as well as for others. He had often felt a mild horror when he heard of a neighbor sinning. He would pray that God continue to spare *him* that pain. שְׁגִיאוֹת מִי יָבִין *(sh'giót mí yavín)*, *Who can understand his errors?* as the psalm said. *Cleanse me from secret faults. Then I shall be righteous, and innocent of all transgression.*

Sexual sin was a mystery to him. He had never been tempted in that way. He found chastity a comfortable state. Most of the young men he knew went to prostitutes. (There were none in Nazareth, but Sepphoris was known for its brothels.) The rabbis had declared this a sin, though there was no express prohibition in the Torah; on the contrary, the patriarch Yehuda, son of Yaakov, had patronized a harlot guiltlessly after his wife had died—a woman he *thought* was a prostitute, though it turned out to be his daughter-in-law, Tamar, and as a result she had given birth to the ancestor of King David and thus to Yosef's own ancestor. But the thought of joining his flesh to the flesh of a depraved woman revolted him. It was a visceral reaction, not a judgment. He didn't consider himself more righteous because of it, nor did he condemn his friends for relieving their bodily needs in that way.

His own temptations were more subtle. They had to do with judgments. We can't help judging, he knew, since that is what the mind does by its very nature. But we can prevent ourselves from acting rashly on these judgments. He was quick to judge his workmen, for example; he hated shoddy work or laziness or stupidity. But he had learned early on from his father to temper his judgments by stepping outside and taking a short walk whenever he needed to reprimand one of the men. By the time he returned to the workshop, he had usually regained his equanimity and was able to point out mistakes and offer suggestions without any notes of harshness or blame. His men said they respected him for that.

When he heard of a neighbor's drunkenness or dishonesty, he tried to be understanding, but again, he often felt a visceral disgust. He never spoke badly of these neighbors—that would be equivalent to disobeying a commandment—but it was a struggle for him to maintain cordial relations with them. He also struggled to be cordial to those who spoke carelessly of God's word

or thought of the law resentfully, as of something imposed on them arbitrarily from the outside. For him,
obeying the commandments was not a matter of cor-
rectness or submission; it was his delight, his life's blood.
He obeyed the commandments with the eagerness of a
schoolboy for whom learning is a passion. The law, to
his eyes, was a thing of surpassing beauty. It was God's
grace. תּוֹרַת יהוה תְּמִימָה *(Torát Adonái t'mimáh), The law of
the Lord is perfect,* he would chant, *refreshing the soul; the
statutes of the Lord are just, rejoicing the heart; the commandments
of the Lord are pure, enlightening the eyes.* What they were for
David, they were for him too: a pathway to freedom,
and it was always a slight shock to him that not every
Jew saw them this way. *More precious are they than gold,* he
would chant, *and sweeter than honey from the honeycomb.*

2.

Let's leave Yosef for a while, as he meditates on Psalm
19, that great hymn to the law and to the freedom
it makes possible. There is nothing abstruse about
God's law, the psalm says; it's available to everyone,
refreshing, rejoicing, enlightening, and making even
the simple wise. The law's beauty is as obvious to the

clear mind as the natural world is. And in the recognition that the heavens declare the glory of God, the sun itself becomes transfigured; it is no longer a material object but a living presence, a figure of power and joy whose rays penetrate everywhere on earth and whose fulfillment is like a human bridegroom's at his wedding or like a champion athlete's at the most intense point of the competition:

> In them is a path for the sun,
>> who steps forth handsome as a bridegroom
>> and rejoices like an athlete as he runs.
> He starts at one end of the heavens
>> and circles to the other end,
> and nothing can hide from his heat.

Contrary to what St. Paul says in his diatribes against the law, there is nothing external about this passionate obedience. "Who can discern his own errors?" the psalmist says. "Cleanse me from hidden faults." It's possible to be free of sin, he goes on to say, by keeping a strict watch on any movement away from righteousness.

> Then I will be blameless,
>> innocent of great transgression.

The Hebrew word translated above as "blame-less" can also mean "perfect," as at the beginning of the Book of Job, where the narrator calls his protagonist "perfect and upright," and the word translated as "innocent" can also mean "without guilt" or "free." That condition, in which the mind of the righteous man or woman rejoices in its freedom from anything that would separate it from God, culminates in the beautiful prayer at the end of the psalm, a request that the psalmist may be permitted to maintain his integrity not only in action but also in the thoughts that are the cause of action:

> May the words of my mouth
> > and the meditation of my heart
> be acceptable in Thy sight, O Lord,
> > my rock and my redeemer.

This is also the point of view of the Epistle of James, which some scholars think was written by James the brother of Jesus, the leader of the early Church in Jerusalem. "Whoever looks carefully into the perfect law that gives freedom, and continues in it," James writes, "not forgetting what he has heard, but actually doing it—he will be blessed in what he does." And then, more precisely:

> What good is it, my brothers, if someone claims to have faith but doesn't show it by his actions? Can that kind of faith save him? Suppose a brother or a sister is poorly clothed and doesn't have enough to eat. If one of you says to them, "Go in peace; keep warm and well fed" but doesn't give them what they need, what good is that? In the same way, faith by itself, if it is not lived out in action, is dead.

So much for the purported opposition between faith and works.

But let's return now to Yosef, as he struggles to be scrupulously righteous in what seems like an impossible situation.

3.

He was in danger of getting trapped in his own harsh judgments. But even if he somehow managed to put aside his anger and sense of betrayal, how could he not be severe with Maryam? Adultery wasn't a casual sin. It was a capital offense—that is, it had once been a capital offense, before the rabbis realized that God's mercy has precedence over the strict language of scripture. There must be a way out of the severity, for his own sake if not for hers. He couldn't stay imprisoned in this bitterness and hatred; it would be the death of him. If he failed to find a way to peace, he would keep gnawing his own heart until … He drew back from imagining how that would end.

He remembered a saying of the great rabbi Hillel, whose fame had spread through all Judea and Galilee: "Do not judge your neighbor until you are in his situation." What was her situation? A comfortable house, loving parents, a loving bridegroom. So what had driven her to sin? Had he been deficient in any way? He searched his memory, but he couldn't come up with a single instance. She had always seemed to be happy with him. She honored him; she adored him—or so she said. She might be a liar, but it wasn't possible for her eyes to tell a lie, was it?

If he had ever been cold or neglectful, he could imagine how a woman might be so upset that she would seek affection elsewhere, in defiance of God's

law. But she would have to be one of those feather-
headed girls who had no experience of God and no
understanding of His commandments—a little nitwit
who didn't realize that charm is deceptive and beauty
is vain. And anyway, it couldn't happen in a small
village like Nazareth, where there were no secrets.
He had heard of girls from Hellenized families, in
cities like Capernaum or Sepphoris, being seduced
by wicked young men (he was ashamed to think
they were Jews) who promised them marriage and
then abandoned them to their shame. Those poor
girls—he could sympathize with them. He could see
how in some ways it was not their fault. They had been
brought up with the wrong values, and they were too
ensnared in their own silly vanity to consider where
their actions would lead them. But Maryam was not
a fool. Whatever she had done to get pregnant, she
couldn't have been seduced. It was out of the question,
unless he had already gone mad and was seeing the
world through the filter of his madness.

What then? It pained him to reason this out, but
there was no other way. He had to get clear about it.
How else could he know the right thing to do? Prayer
might help, but he had prayed already, as much as
he could for now. Perhaps God would be gracious

enough later to let him see more clearly. In the meantime, he had to go step by step, on his own, and think things through for himself. In some way, in any way he could find, he had to crawl out of this intolerable confusion.

If, then, she had not been seduced, there were only two possibilities. She might have been raped. This was a rare occurrence in Nazareth, but it wasn't unheard of. Women seldom went alone in public places; they usually walked to the well or to the market in pairs, arm in arm. When there was a rape, it was of a woman working alone in the fields or walking from field to farmhouse, and the culprit was usually a drunken farmer or one of Herod's brutal soldiers from the garrison at Sepphoris. The law was unequivocal. In the case of a betrothed woman, the rapist was put to death and the woman didn't become prohibited to her husband—unless, of course, he was a priest, which Yosef, being of the tribe of Judah, wasn't, thank God.

Could this have happened to Maryam? It was improbable. She would have let him know. And even a girl of her natural composure would have been distraught if she had been raped. Yet when she had told him the news, she had looked calm, not like a woman who has just gone through an experience of horror. She had seemed a bit anxious at first, true, but when she had mentioned her pregnancy she had smiled. But what if the attack had unbalanced her mind? Was that possible? Could it have devastated her to such an extent that she had buried it in her memory and hallucinated an encounter with an angel? Perhaps she wasn't lying. Perhaps she truly believed that such an encounter had happened.

However unlikely this was, he had to consider the possibility. If she really had been raped, he would without question take her home as his wife and become a father to her child. His heart would ache for her, and he would do everything in his power to nurse her back to health. And if she didn't recover from her madness, he would care for her as for a beloved child with an incurable illness. His earnings were enough that he could afford to hire a woman who would look after both mother and child. Maryam would, however, have to testify in court that she had been raped. If she persisted in telling the story about the angel, the judges would assume that she was lying in an attempt to cover up her adultery, and he would be obligated by law to divorce her. Nor could he simply take her home and keep the matter hidden. The fact that the child was a bastard had to be made public. It would be a grave injustice to hide that from the community. According to the law, a bastard was not to enter the congregation of the Lord, even to the tenth generation. If he kept silent about the child's origin, he would be committing a sin against the family whose child the bastard married, God forbid. People needed to know, so that they could avoid ritual pollution.

The second possibility, which seemed even more far-fetched, was that Maryam was telling the truth about a meeting with an angel. No one had seen one for five hundred years—not since the prophet Zechariah spoke comfortably with an angel who stood among the myrtle trees, in the second year of Darius the Great. That didn't mean that it couldn't have happened to Maryam. She was an extraordinary woman. Could she have been impregnated by an angel? Everyone knew that in the time of Noah, two thousand years before, the sons of God had seen that the daughters of men were beautiful, and they had made love to any of them they chose. The rabbis said that these "sons of God" were members of the lowest rank in the angelic hierarchy, a rank peculiarly susceptible to physical beauty, even though they were nonphysical beings. The angels were themselves so radiantly beautiful in the fleshly forms they assumed, the rabbis said, that no woman on earth, not even the most virtuous, had been able to resist their advances. If this was what had happened to Maryam, there could be no blame.

But it put him in a difficult position. If there was no blame, then there was no seduction, and the case was analogous to rape. But the judges would never be able to countenance this possibility, and in any case the child would still be a bastard, which would eliminate the option of keeping the matter out of court. In addition, the child might very well turn out to be a giant, as in the days of Noah—one of the offspring of those angels, the *nephilim*, the "mighty men of old," who had supernatural strength, psychic powers, and twelve fingers and toes. The extra fingers and toes would be apparent as soon as the child was born. In that case, there would of course be no need to verify her account.

He suddenly became aware of a restlessness in his legs. He rose from the chair, stood up, and paced back and forth, to his work table, to the front door, then back to the table. So many thoughts swirled through his mind that he could barely grasp any one of them. He poured out some water, dipped his hands into the basin, wet his face, dried it, and sat back down.

His head had cleared now, as though he had awoken from a dream. How could he have been so gullible

as to consider those two possibilities? She had been seduced: that must have been what had happened. She
was a naïve girl, and some unscrupulous rich man
had come from the city and seduced her, and she was
so mortified at what she had done that she had made
up the story about the angel. He pitied her. But he
would have to give her up. He had no choice. The law
was clear. Her crime was not his problem, nor was
the bastard child. Why should he miss his chance for
a happy family? He would have to cut her off, the way
a surgeon cuts off a diseased limb.

There was only one option, then: divorce. God
was not calling on him to marry Maryam, as He
had laid His command upon the prophet Hosea:
"Go now, marry a whore and have bastard children." As much as he pitied her, as miserable as her
prospects were after the divorce, he would have to
steel his heart against her and go through with the
legal process. He would not, of course, shame her in
public by bringing her before a tribunal. He would
simply draft a writ of repudiation. In this way, he
would not be obliged to state his reasons for the divorce. The School of Hillel, with its lenient point of
view, prevailed in most districts, and according to
its interpretation of the law, any act on the part of

the wife or the betrothed woman that displeased a man—even if she only burned a meal—was reason enough to divorce her. This leniency was meant to protect the woman as well as the man from a loveless marriage, since any man who blamed a woman so severely was not fit to be her husband. Since there would be no accusation, there would be no immediate disgrace for Maryam. But as the months passed and her pregnancy began to show, people would naturally connect it with the divorce; there was no way around that. He considered having the wedding first and not divorcing her until afterward, but that was impossible. It might save her reputation, but only at the cost of breaking the law, since the child would be considered legitimate and would grow up to pollute some decent, God-fearing family.

The sun had set by now. He got up and walked out the door. There was a sliver of moon in the sky, and as he walked down the main street of the village in the thickening twilight, he felt relieved that no one was about. He turned a corner, and in two minutes he arrived at his house. He felt more exhausted than he had ever been in his life. He undressed quickly, got into bed, and immediately fell asleep.

The angel who appeared to Yosef in his dream

looked like a young man, though his cheeks were as smooth and pink as a girl's. Six inches above his head, a thin golden halo hovered like an enormous wedding ring. His golden hair was parted in the middle and fell to his shoulders in soft curls. He was wearing a rose-colored silk robe, cinched with a belt of interlocking gold clasps. His wings were hawks' wings, tapering at the tips, each successive row of feathers a different color—purple, blue, green, yellow, red. The wings flapped once in salutation, then slowly folded onto his back. He looked at Yosef with fierce green animal-eyes.

"Yosef," he said, "do not be afraid to take Maryam as your wife, for the child in her has been begotten through the Holy Spirit. And she will give birth to a son, and you shall name him Yeshua, for he will save his people from their sins." As Yosef heard this message, he shuddered and awoke.

4.

For Yosef's angel, I have borrowed the hair, robe, and multicolored wings that Fra Angelico gave Gabriel in his portrait of the Annunciation. The "fierce green animal-eyes" are my own invention. This angel too, in spite of his elegant Renaissance trappings, is terrifying.

But even an angel with a comfortable outward form might bring a terrifying message. Raphael, for example, the archangel of healing in the apocryphal book of Tobit, stands in front of the hero, Tobias, in the form of a human being, a young man so ordinary-looking that Tobias has no idea he is an angel. I can imagine Raphael coming to Yosef in this form, in Yosef's waking consciousness, with a message of just two words: "Trust her."

But these two simple words, which strip the situation of all its complexities, would seem terrifying to Yosef, because they would eliminate his sense of control. The sense of control is one of the strengths of religious systems, and it is a powerful motivation to righteousness, which is another name for decency and kindness. But it is also a weakness, because ultimately it's untrue. And when you believe that you're in control, you can easily fall into the illusion of *doing* and let your inner life become a business enterprise: if I do such and such, then God has to do such and such in return; that is, if I obey all the commandments and keep to the letter of the law, then God is obligated to reward me with spiritual goodies, such as entrance into heaven.

But if I trust my beloved with all my heart, that sense of control is no longer possible, and the thought "I am right" isn't sustainable. Everything I believe—any thought that separates me from her—has to be questioned, so that I can come into alignment with her. Otherwise, I condemn myself to confusion and suffering. This is the end of my precious identity as I have known it. No wonder that "Trust her" would be a terrifying sentence to hear.

Matthew's angel is ostensibly kinder. "Marry her" offers Yosef clear direction, which he can certainly follow. The explanation, that "the child has been begotten through the Holy Spirit," is a remarkably vague one, and it would give Yosef a lot to contemplate—mental activity that might helpfully diminish his terror. Is "begotten" being used metaphorically, as in Psalm 2, where David (or an anonymous psalmist) says, "The Lord said to me, 'You are my son; this day I have begotten you'"? (In other words, "The Lord said to me, 'Today, at the age of [fill in the blank], you have been spiritually begotten, you have become a child of God.'") Or is the verb being used with its literal meaning, "to procreate as a father," or more explicitly, "to ejaculate into a vagina so that one of the sperm unites with an egg and produces a human child"? In the second option, God couldn't have been the baby's father unless He had a penis, though the father could conceivably have been an angel, as for example with the "mighty men of old" at the beginning of Genesis, who were begotten by the "sons of God" upon the daughters of men.

But eventually Yosef would have to confront the actual choice. Should he trust Maryam or trust himself? What is the validity of his initial reaction to the news? How can he expand his thinking so that there is nothing left in his heart but love?

5.

Yosef sat up in bed. What did it mean? Was the dream from God? In scripture, angels never appear with a message in a dream. It is God who brings messages in dreams; angels always deliver their messages in waking time. But certainly the dream was no ordinary dream. He closed his eyes and tried to re-enter it, but the image of the angel had already faded; he could no longer remember it. He felt a pang of longing, as though he had been stabbed through the heart by sweetness.

He couldn't remember the angel's face, but he

remembered his words: "Do not be afraid to take Maryam as your wife." So: that, at least, was settled. He had to complete the second step of the marriage, the *nisu'in*, and by taking Maryam to live with him, declare that she was his wife. There would be no divorce. He didn't have a choice. God had commanded this.

His heart rebelled for a moment. Was he to be another Hosea? No, Maryam couldn't be a whore, not if her pregnancy had been commanded by the Lord. She had to be innocent. But innocent in what way? The dream angel had said that the child had been begotten in her through the Holy Spirit. *Through* didn't necessarily mean agency; it could also mean permission, as in "with the blessing of the Holy Spirit, God's manifestation on earth." That must mean that God had *wanted* her to commit adultery. It was God's will that she conceive the child out of wedlock. This was painful to contemplate. But it was clear that for some reason, known only to the Almighty in His infinite wisdom, her adultery had been necessary. Yosef would not presume to argue with God. He would have to accept this. Whether the child had a human or an angel as his father, it was blessed, even though it was a bastard, because it had been begotten at the directive—or with the acquiescence—of the Holy Spirit. In either case, the law about bastards too must not apply. So in keeping silent about the child's origin, Yosef would not be sinning against any of his neighbors. And if he took Maryam home with him right away, everyone would believe that the child was his. When the boy grew up, Yosef would, in good conscience, be able to arrange a marriage for him.

His thoughts returned to Maryam and the father of her child. He was mortified that God had made him a cuckold, whether it had been by means of a man or an angel. It was ridiculous. It was demeaning. But he realized that his shame was simply the outer crust of the pride that for so many years he had been praying to grow beyond. This must be another test. He would have to surrender his will to God. He would have to see that this was the best thing that could have happened to him and to Maryam. If he was sincere in his devotion, his wounded masculine pride would be a trivial sacrifice. He could offer it up as easily as a priest slits the throat of a lamb at the altar.

What was it that the angel had said about the child? "You shall name him Yeshua, for he will save his people from their sins." What could that mean? Some sort of greatness was being held in store for the child, and that made the humiliation more bearable. If the boy became a great rabbi, how petty it would be to care about who his father was! Yosef could even bless the man in his heart—or the angel. A son of his own flesh, after all, would probably never amount to anything more than an ordinary village craftsman like himself. Perhaps this boy would even, by his teachings, hasten the coming of the kingdom of God. Isaiah had prophesied the sign by which the Messiah would be recognized: "Behold, the young woman shall conceive and bear a son and shall name him Immanuel."* So Maryam's little Yeshua might even be the harbinger of the long-awaited Immanuel. If Immanuel came to establish God's kingdom on earth, how laughable this hurt pride would seem when Yosef looked back at it from the reality of that glorious kingdom!

Still, he was troubled. He knew that he would have to forgive her completely if he was truly going to be her husband. He had practiced forgiveness all his life; it was a central part of his piety. When people who had sinned against him had repented and made amends and sincerely begged his forgiveness, he had always for-

---

* The Hebrew means "God [Is] With Us."

given them, as he was morally bound to do. But was "forgiveness" the appropriate word here? Maryam had acknowledged nothing. Perhaps she hadn't sinned. The truth was that he didn't know what had happened. He knew that the child had been blessed by the Holy Spirit—nothing more than that. Perhaps she really had been visited by an angel, and the angel had not actually begotten the child but only touched her with his finger or with his mind. Perhaps the dream angel had used "begotten" not in its literal sense but meta-phorically, as in Psalm 2. How could he know that it had happened any differently than that? And if so, was there anything to forgive?

He could not and would not believe the impossi-ble; this was a matter of integrity for him. But he knew that the possible was vaster than anything he was capable of knowing. There had been great miracles among his people in the past, and why should there not be another miracle now, especially if Maryam's son was to be the precursor to Immanuel, the longed-for Messiah? He could accept that he himself was not righteous enough to be the father of a son like that. Maryam herself could provide all the righteousness the child would ever need.

Trying to figure out what might or might not

have happened wearied him. God alone knew—and Maryam. The only thing he could know was that this inner separation from her was excruciating. He couldn't even remember exactly what she had said to him, only that an angel had come to her and that she was pregnant. Had she told him how it had happened? Did he need to know?

Before the news, he had never felt any sense of separation from her, ever since the moment he had met her. There was much about her that he was unable to fully understand: her transparency, the depth of her soul. But the disproportion between her and him hadn't affected their intimacy. He had always felt as loved by her as it is possible for a human being to be loved. Looking into her eyes was like seeing himself in a mirror that reflected back his own face, more beautiful than he could ever have imagined.

Since yesterday, that intimacy had been shattered. The separation was too painful to be borne. He would do anything to end it. He found himself praying again. חָנֵּנִי אֱלֹהִים כְּחַסְדֶּךָ *(Hanéyni, Elohím, k'hasdékha), Have mercy upon me, O God, according to Your lovingkindness. Wash me from my iniquity and cleanse me from my sin.* It was a psalm he knew well from the liturgy, but he had never used it in his private devotions. He chanted it without even knowing what iniquity he was asking forgiveness for. But as soon as he looked inside himself, the iniquity was obvious. It was his anger at Maryam, his distrust, his willingness to put pride before justice. He had leaped to the harshest of conclusions without even going back to speak with her. *Be the listener*: the words were whispered in some far corner of his mind. Was this another message from God? He had not really listened to Maryam. Rather than hearing her account of what had happened, he had turned away from her to enter a world of his own brooding. It had been a transgression against their love. *Wash me*, he prayed, *and I shall be whiter than snow. Make me hear joy and gladness, that the bones Thou hast broken may rejoice. Do not cast me away from Thy presence; do not take Thy Holy Spirit from me.*

But it was not enough to ask for God's forgiveness. He would need to ask for Maryam's forgiveness as well, since she was the one he had sinned against. He had no fear about doing this. He knew how she would react. She would listen to him with love shining from her eyes, and she would say, "Of course I forgive you, my heart. But don't you know that there's nothing to forgive?" And it would be over. It would be as though no separation had ever happened, as though there had never been any sin since the creation of the world.

That was how she always reacted. If she was not offended, then there could be no offense. He would need to resemble her in that. There could be no lingering hurt or upset in his mind. Even the faintest reverberation of an upset would separate him from her, and he wouldn't be able to bear that. He vowed that whatever might be the difficulties they were to face in their life together, he would not pull back from her again. If he ever felt that happening, he would tell her. He wanted not only the words of his mouth but the meditation of his heart to be open before her, to be worthy of her.

He could see that all the agitation and despair of yesterday had come from his lack of trust. It had nothing to do with her. She was as innocent as she had been the day before and the day before that. It was his own hurt pride, superimposed onto her—his own thinking—that had created the dreadful barrier between them. And without that thinking, he could see her again as the blessed one, the destined one, the love of his life, the mother of his children, except for the firstborn. It could all return to what it used to be. It already had returned.

The realization brought tears to his eyes. It was

as though he had just emerged from the ritual bath before Friday night prayers at the synagogue. He felt fresh and invigorated, as though he was ready to ascend the mountain of the Lord and to stand in His holy place with clean hands and a pure heart, and the gates had lifted up their heads, and the everlasting doors, and the King of glory had entered.

He found himself, to his great surprise, rejoicing that she was pregnant. It was as much an occasion for rejoicing as though he himself were the father. He remembered the smile on her face when she had told him the news.

He would adopt the child. There would be no need to do this legally, and indeed it must not be done in public. He would adopt the child in his heart. He would love him as though he were his own son. He would teach him his trade and help him become an excellent craftsman, one for whom the quality of his work was a measure of his devotion to the Lord. And when the boy was old enough, he would teach him the holy tongue, so that he could read God's word directly. He would sit the boy on his lap and teach him the letters: *aleph*, an ox head, *bet*, a house, *gimel*, a camel, each letter in the alphabet as sweet as honey from the honeycomb. He would show him by his own example what it meant to be righteous, insofar as he could do that. He would take his little hand in his own hand and guide him on the path that he himself had been guided on. And later, the boy, like his father, would delight in the law of the Lord, and in His law he would meditate day and night.

He thought of Maryam again, and he could barely contain his excitement. He would take her home soon: no, today. He would care for her over the next nine months, and he would not sleep with her until after she had given birth to her firstborn. They would love each other in every child she gave birth to. Yes, the firstborn son would be special and would grow up to be an extraordinary man, a great hero in Israel. But each of their children would be special. Each would be the fruit of their love, and each would be loved equally.

He could see her face now as it had looked when she appeared to him yesterday. No wonder there was that hint of anxiety on her features. If only he had understood then what he understood now! But it didn't matter. He had come back to her. It was a new beginning.

He heard chanting in the back of his mind: the Song of Songs, in its beautiful cantillation. ‏קוּמִי לָךְ

רַעְיָתִי יָפָתִי *(Kúmi lákh, rayatí, yafatí)*, Arise, my beloved, my beauty, and come away with me now. For look, the winter is past; the rains are over and gone; flowers have appeared on the earth; the time of the songbirds has come, and the voice of the turtledove is heard in our land; the fig tree ripens with fruit; the grapevines pour forth their fragrance. Arise, my beloved, my beauty, and come away with me now.

It was morning: a new day. He got out of bed, dressed, and walked out into the street. He could feel his heart pounding. In a few minutes he would be standing at her door.

Interlude

IN LUKE'S NATIVITY STORY, Joseph is mentioned only peripherally. Mary is the focus there; Joseph is hardly a character at all. Matthew, on the other hand, puts him at the center of the legend. The story is extremely compressed:

> [Mary's] husband, Joseph, was a righteous man and was unwilling to expose her to public disgrace, so he decided to divorce her in private. But as he was considering this, an angel appeared to him in a dream and said, "Joseph, son of David, do not be afraid to take Mary as your wife," etc. When Joseph awoke from his sleep, he did as the angel had commanded him, and he married her and took her home with him as his wife, but he did not have sex with her until she had given birth to her firstborn son.

It's the bare minimum; the story is over before we know it, before we've had a chance to grasp the moral greatness of its hero. And because Matthew, like Luke, writes in such a concise form, he makes Joseph's yes seem as easy as Mary's yes to Gabriel. But when we pay closer attention, we become aware of the precise nature of Joseph's dilemma and of his triumph.

I wrote the passage about Yosef's angel, with his "fierce green animal-eyes," a while ago, but I just this moment realized that there is an ironic resonance with *Othello*, where Iago calls jealousy "the green-eyed monster." Hmm. It could be that my angel is the transformed, resplendent creature jealousy becomes after you have experienced total trust in the beloved.

Othello, as it happens, is the deepest, most horrifying treatment of jealousy that we have in our literature. Wordsworth spoke of it as one of the three "most pathetic of human compositions," and Swinburne, in one of his fussy phrases, called Othello "the noblest man of man's making." He is certainly noble in his professional life, but in his personal life? Not so much. The more he's consumed by the mounting evidence—the *apparent* evidence—of Desdemona's unfaithfulness, the more he shows how little he understands who she is and how shallow he is in his understanding of himself. True nobility, according to the dictionary, is "superiority of mind or of character; commanding moral worth or excellence," and Othello lacks this in his most important human relationship. True, Desdemona sees him as noble, but she is just seeing her projected version of him: "my noble Moor / Is true of mind and made of no such baseness / As jealous creatures are." If only. In her case, innocence is blind and trust is lethal.

Even a genius of a villain wouldn't be able to infect the mind of someone who is deeply rooted in his love for his wife. And the fatal handkerchief? Any sensible husband, even if he were so unconscious as to let himself get entangled in suspicions, would go to his wife and discover the truth.

"What happened to the handkerchief I gave you?"

"I don't know, sweetheart. I have no idea how I could have lost it. I'm so sorry. I know how much you value it. I've looked for it everywhere, all over the house. But maybe it will still turn up."

Her sincerity would be obvious, and he would believe her. But then there would be no tragedy, which is what Shakespeare set out to write.

Jealousy is a mode of ignorance. It's one of the most painful emotions a human can experience. Othello is destroyed by it, but Yosef finds a way out, a way through. In Matthew's story, it takes a visit from an angel to turn him around. What would it take to turn you around?

6

The Wise Men

However men try to reach Me,
I return their love with My love;
whatever path they may travel,
it leads to Me in the end.

—BHAGAVAD GITA

✳

1.

ACCORDING TO LEGENDS that sprang up centuries after the Gospels were written, the wise men came from Persia; there were three of them, each with an exotic Eastern name. They were not only wise men but kings, the legends say, and they kneeled at the manger clothed in velvet, silk, and ermine, bearing gifts of unimaginable splendor, their bright-colored turbans bedecked with jewels and the feathers of rare birds, their heads encircled by golden haloes the size of dinner plates. Simple piety invented these details to honor the newborn child. But the truth is quite different.

There were only two wise men. Though they came to Bethlehem from India, far to the east, they were Jews. Their names were Eleazar bar Shimon and Yehuda bar Gamaliel ha-Levi. They were scions of prominent Judean families and disciples of the great rabbi Hillel the Elder. Seventeen years before, they had left Jerusalem and traveled to the Malabar Coast with his blessing. Here's how it happened.

The two had begun to study Torah with Hillel when they were boys, eager to learn from the greatest Jewish sage and jurist of his time. Hillel was an excellent teacher, and he had trained two generations of rabbis in his meticulous, compassionate interpretation of the law. Many of his sayings expressed a practical and psychologically astute wisdom, and in the inner circle of his disciples (our two young men entered it when they were twenty-one) everyone used these sayings as themes for contemplation. The most famous was "Whatever is unpleasant to you, do not do to your neighbor. That is the whole Torah; the rest is commentary. Go now and learn." The second most famous was "If I am not for myself, who will be for me? And if I am for myself alone, what am I? And if not now, when?" This second saying the disciples divided into three parts; they would spend a week at a time contemplating each part and a fourth week contemplating the intricacies of how the three parts fit together and how each illuminated the others.

By the time Eleazar and Yehuda had reached the age of thirty, in the year 21 BCE, Hillel, at eighty-nine, was too frail to keep up his teaching schedule and had retired to a life of contemplation and prayer. Neither of the men felt drawn to study with any of his first- or second-generation disciples. It was not that they didn't respect them; they just didn't have the kind of passionate affinity with these disciples that they had with the Master. They had heard rumors that there were enlightened teachers in India, teachers who had never heard of the Torah but had somehow acquired a wisdom that surpassed even the wisdom of Solomon. There had been Jews in India for five hundred years, ever since Judean traders had settled in the Hindu kingdom of Cochin and been given permission to live freely, build synagogues, and own property "for as long as the earth and the moon shall endure." The intention of Eleazar and Yehuda was to travel there in order to find a deeply enlightened teacher.

When they told Hillel of their idea, he tried to

dissuade them. Wasn't it arrogant, he asked, to think that there was no one among all his disciples who was worthy of becoming their teacher? The two men said that they were sure they could profit in many ways from one of the Master's senior disciples and that they understood the Master's warning that "he who does not increase his knowledge decreases it." But their wish to go to India had nothing to do with knowledge; it had to do with wisdom. The Master's wisdom was what they longed for, and if they could sit at his feet for the next 120 years, it would be like sitting in the Garden of Eden and feeding on the fruit of the Tree of Life. One saying of the Master's in particular had been the subject of their contemplation in recent years: "If I am here, everyone is here; if I am not here, no one is here." They had made little progress with this saying. They could see how it applied to God, whose true name, as revealed to Moses from the burning bush, is *I am.* But they had not been able to find a way to apply the saying to themselves, and their most ardent desire was to understand it on all levels and then to live it, if only they could find a way to penetrate to its depths.

Hillel looked at them for a long time with love and sadness in his eyes. Then he said that he understood, and he gave them his blessing. May they find what they were searching for, wherever they could find it. He asked them, however, to promise him one thing: not to separate themselves from the Jewish community. They promised. The next day they left for India.

The Jews of Cochin were horrified at their intention. No, no, they said, Hindus were idol worshipers. Doing business with them was permitted but not for one moment should a Jew be exposed to their doctrines, which were nothing but blasphemy and madness. There were thousands of Hindu gods, they said, and worshipers chose among them as though they were shopping for bargains at a village fair. Everyone had his pet deity, whom he sacrificed to and begged for favors, and all of them were false gods, mere imagination, direct affronts to the Creator, blessed be He, who had expressly forbidden the worship of any god but Himself. It was shameful even to mention it, but there was a whole panoply of monsters in the Hindu pantheon: three-headed gods; blue-skinned gods; gods with a human body and the head of an elephant or ape; female gods with tiny waists, provocative hips, and pornographic breasts; gods of fire and water, thunder and lightning, sun and moon; dark gods of the underworld;

gigantic gods whose footstep could crush a village; diminutive gods the size of beetles or ants; gods who manifested themselves in every atrocious form that the human imagination could invent; even gods who took the form of the phallus or the female genitalia, and one could only imagine what practices went on behind the doors of the temples where these abominations were worshiped.

Eleazar and Yehuda listened to the Jews of Cochin respectfully and thanked them for their advice. Then they went on their way in search of an enlightened Master.

They traveled from town to town in southern India, occasionally selling one of the small diamonds they had sewn into the hems of their garments, learning the Tamil language as they went, and enough of the local dialects to be understood by the villagers. Wherever they went, they were the only light-skinned people amid a sea of dark-brown faces, and more than once they thought of the verse from the Song of Songs in which the Shulamite says, שְׁחוֹרָה אֲנִי וְנָאוָה (Shḥoráh aní v'na'váh), *I am black and beautiful, O daughters of Jerusalem.*

As they proceeded, they were recommended to dozens of spiritual teachers, each of whom was, according to his devotees, a fully enlightened Master. Each turned out to be a sham. Some were scholars who had memorized the Vedas and Upanishads and could find a scriptural verse for every occasion but whose pomposity and self-satisfaction immediately disqualified them in the eyes of the two seekers. Others were mystics, wild men who had undergone severe ascetic practices for decades—staring at the sun until they were blind, or hanging upside down from the branch of a sacred oak, or subsisting on nothing but cow urine, or sitting cross-legged in mountain caves until their finger- and toenails had grown as long as their forearms—and each had emerged with the ability to perform miracles or to act as the authorized mouthpiece of the divine. But however fascinating these teachers were, they didn't speak with anything that Eleazar and Yehuda could recognize as wisdom. Some of them turned out to be closed-hearted; others took pride in their intelligence or their spiritual accomplishments or the number of devotees who flocked to hear them; still others preached celibacy and had secret concubines. After a short time with each, the two men would leave to continue their search.

One day they stopped for lunch in a small town called Tiruvannamalai, about 240 miles to the northeast of Cochin. The inn served a buffet meal, and when they had helped themselves to a selection of the dairy and vegetable dishes and sat down, a waitress came to their table, took their order for drinks (one lemonade, one mangoade), and then, in a friendly, curious tone, asked why they had come to India. Eleazar told her. "Ah, an enlightened Master," she said. "Well, go see the fellow who runs the laundry shop. They call him Bodhananda."

Bodhananda was a short, thin man of about fifty with luminous eyes and a cheerfulness that seemed to bubble up out of him like an underground spring. He was standing at the counter between two large piles of soiled clothing. "What can I do for you, young gentlemen?" he said. He spoke pure Tamil.

"Someone suggested that we come see you," Yehuda said.

"Have you brought me any dirty laundry?"

"No, sir," said Eleazar.

"Really!" Bodhananda said with a raised eyebrow and an expression of vast amusement.

"We are looking for wisdom," Yehuda said. "We have traveled a very great distance to be here."

"Our scriptures," Eleazar said, "ask the question

'Where shall wisdom be found?' We long to answer that question. That is why we have come to India."

"So you are seekers," Bodhananda said.

"Yes, sir."

"Well, this wisdom you speak of, young gentlemen, will never be found by seeking." He paused for a moment. "Yet only seekers can find it."

Eleazar and Yehuda exchanged a quick, excited glance. Then Yehuda said, "We would like to study with you, sir, if you will accept us as your students."

"Study with me? Accept you as my students?" Bodhananda said. "Bring me your dirty laundry!" Then he shooed them out the door.

They walked through the streets in a daze. "I felt as though I were in a room filled with laughter," Eleazar said.

"Yes," Yehuda said. "I felt that way too. Did you ever see eyes like his? The light in them! I know that he knows."

"I had the same thought. Not only has he seen the answer, he has become it."

"I felt as though I could walk straight into those eyes, for miles and miles, and at the end of them I would meet myself."

Eleazar nodded.

The next day, the two men went back to Bodh-ananda's shop with two armfuls of soiled tunics and underclothes. He burst into laughter and shooed them out the door.

Undaunted, they returned every day. Bodh-ananda allowed them to sit with him for a few minutes each time, then told them to leave.

One day Yehuda said, "Before you dismiss us, sir, please answer one question, which has been troubling me ever since I was thirteen years old."

"Yes?"

"Why does God permit evil in the world?"

"Ah," said Bodhananda with a chuckle. "Some dirty laundry at last!" Then he shooed them out the door.

The next day, when they came to the shop, there was a small short-legged circular table set in front of the counter with three cushions around it. On one cushion sat Bodhananda. A teapot and three cups were clustered in the center of the table, and as soon as the men entered, he poured the pungent, auburn-colored tea and asked them to sit down.

"Where do you come from?" Bodhananda said.

"From a land far to the west of here," Yehuda said. "It is called Judea, and our holy city is Jerusalem."

Bodhananda raised an eyebrow. Then, again, he asked, a bit more slowly, "Where do you come from?"

"Oh," Yehuda said, embarrassed. "We come from God, the source of all things."

"Are you sure of that?" Bodhananda said.

Both men vigorously nodded their assent.

"If you are serious about knowing the truth," Bodhananda said, "you mustn't be sure of anything. I see you have the God sickness. Other people arrive here with the no-God sickness. It doesn't matter. It all comes out in the wash." He reached for his cup.

As they drank their tea, he continued. "All answers are already inside you. You don't need to look anywhere else. Even the greatest teachers can do nothing more than point the way. It is a figure of speech to say that you can learn wisdom from anyone. You can learn it only from yourself. If it is worth attaining, it has already been attained."

"But will you help us, sir?" Eleazar said.

"Yes, if you are willing," Bodhananda said. "I

have been able to do that once or twice before. I prescribe medicine for the sickness, then I prescribe antidotes for the medicine, then antidotes for the antidotes, until finally the unconfused student says, 'Thank you very much, but that's enough. I am perfectly well now.'"

So began their seventeen years of meditation practice in India.

2.

Bodhananda had different methods for different students. He took atheists on the path of faith until eventually there were able to see reality itself as God and everyone they met as a form of the beloved. Theists he took on the path of doubt. Question everything you believe, he told them, whether it is a belief about God, the world, or yourself. Beliefs are always obstacles to the God beyond "God," and the more fiercely you find yourself wanting to defend a belief, the bigger an obstacle it is likely to be. Eventually, when all beliefs have been questioned and seen through, what you have been seeking will manifest itself in all its splendor.

This path, he would say, is like a circle with four principal points on it. People in total ignorance are situated at the 0° point. Moving upward to the right along the circumference, we arrive at 90°, the place of knowledge, the point where you find scholars, philosophers, and theologians—all those who know something or think that they do. The 180° point, at the top, is the place of emptiness, where nothing at all exists and there is neither knowing nor not-knowing, since no one exists to either know or not-know. At 270°, practitioners attain supernormal powers. This is the point of miracles and magic, where people may gain the ability to become invisible, walk on water, read minds, see the future, pass through walls, change water into wine, or fly through the air without wings. But these powers are always a hindrance to spiritual progress, and the practitioner must be careful never to wish or summon them but to experience them only as they spontaneously arise; he must ride out this phase until the powers drop off from him naturally, like ripe fruit from a tree. The final point is at the bottom, 360°, which is exactly the same point as 0°, except that you have come full circle. Instead of ignorance, you find yourself in the place of unknowing, the don't-know mind, which doesn't believe any of the thoughts that pass through it, and thus is completely open to reality and can love whatever happens to you, however bad or good it might seem. When you have arrived at this 360° point, Bodhananda would say, looking to the holy books would be like thirsting for water when you are neck-deep in water. As the scriptures themselves say:

> When your understanding has passed
> beyond the thicket of delusions,
> there is nothing you need to learn
> from even the most sacred scripture.

This is freedom. You are left as pure presence, like all natural creatures, standing upright and joyous in the only moment that has ever existed.

Eleazar and Yehuda took it upon themselves to dive into the practice of meditation under the Master's guidance. They began with the elementary method of counting their breaths, then after six months moved to simply observing their breaths, then after another year they did away with even that prop and immersed themselves in choiceless awareness.

Five and a half years later, after many ups and many downs, Yehuda had a breakthrough. Sitting cross-legged on a cushion in their rented room, he suddenly felt weightless, bodiless. The whole world had disappeared. There were no thoughts left in his mind and no thinker. It was like being plunged, awake, into a state of dreamless sleep. How long the experience lasted he didn't know; it could have been five seconds or five hours. When he returned to normal consciousness, his legs were asleep, and as he tried to stand up, they almost collapsed beneath him. Afterward, he noticed that the question about evil, which had tortured him for a dozen years, had entirely disappeared. It had been answered with a completeness beyond anything he could have hoped for. He no longer had any concepts about God. The word *God* itself seemed like an echoing seashell.

He also noticed a lightheartedness inside him that he had never experienced before as an adult. When he went for a walk in the countryside, he felt like Adam in paradise, naming every plant and animal for the first time. This large many-branched green-covered creature: tree. That deep-blue expanse overhead: sky. But he could just as easily have reversed the names and called the blue expanse tree and the many-branched creature sky. In themselves they didn't have names, and without names they were not separate from each other or from himself. Nothing was separate. It was all part of the same continuous reality. There was no life and no death. There was only the one! the one! And not even that, not even one, there was nothing! And not even nothing, since to say "nothing" is to make it a something. Words collapsed as soon as you put any pressure on them. For days he found himself in a state of continual amazement.

When he told Bodhananda what had happened, the Master patted him on the head. "Good, good," he said. "But keep going. These are just baby steps."

It took Eleazar another two years to reach a similar point of expansion. For him it felt like a death. It seemed to him that he had lost everything that had given meaning to his life. It was as though a fire had swept through his inner landscape and left it ravaged, with all its houses and gardens burned to the ground and nothing left but the smoldering ashes. He had been suddenly transported from his own comfortable mind into the mind of Ecclesiastes. "'Emptiness, pure emptiness,' says the Teacher. 'What can a man gain by all his toil under the sun? There is no remembrance of those who came before us, and there will be no remembrance of those who come after.'" Never in his life had he felt so desolate, so afraid.

When he told Bodhananda of all this, the Master said, "Good. The ego hates to have its little tricks uncovered. But who is it who is desolate? Meditate on that."

After three weeks the fear settled down, then vanished. The desolation in Eleazar's heart began to seem like something positive and natural, like a tree losing its leaves and standing, fully exposed, to face the oncoming winter. Of *course* past and future had to fall away, he realized, if he was to draw closer to the God who, in the words of Ecclesiastes, has made everything beautiful in its own time and has put eternity in our heart.

He began to have 270° experiences in the ninth year. Sometimes during his meditation periods he saw angels. They had the faces of human children, innocent and beautiful beyond description. They would stare at him with unblinking eyes, never saying a word. One of them, once, smiled and put its fingers to its lips. When he came out of the meditation, his heart ached with the beauty of these angels.

At other times he found himself inside a vortex, hurtling toward a tiny, brilliant point of light. When he stepped out into the brilliance, he was embraced by all his beloved dead—his five-year-old sister, Rebecca; his grandparents; two of his boyhood friends who had died in the cholera epidemic; and even some of the great men of ancient times: King Solomon, the prophet Micah, the scholar Antigonus of Sokho.

During one meditation period, he found himself in two places at the same moment. It was bizarre. He was having a conversation with Yehuda in Aramaic, sitting in their room in Tiruvannamalai, and he was also speaking in Tamil to an Indian pilgrim on a slope of Arunachala Mountain. He could feel his arms resting on the small wooden table and could see Yehuda and the yellow-painted plaster wall behind him and, simultaneously, facing the white-robed pilgrim, he could smell the vegetation on the mountainside, pungent after the rain. All the while the two conversations wove in and out of each other like two lines of counterpoint.

Another time, he was suddenly a hawk, soaring down from the clouds toward a pond a mile away, with the air rushing through his feathers and his eyes trained on a mallard that floated on the water far below. As he swooped, a fierce shriek exploded from his throat, and it was all he could do to retract his claws and at the last moment pull himself, terrified, up and away from the terrified duck.

Toward the end of their fourteenth year in India,

Yehuda had several experiences of this sort. There was a drought in the Tamil land that had continued for months during the season when the crops desperately needed rain. The thought of starving children moved him to pray for rain as fervently as Honi the Circle-Drawer had prayed for it a generation before. It was not that he was asking God to do anything; it was a matter of pure intention, the rain in his mind dropping down from the heavens like tears of compassion. He prayed the whole of a morning and halfway into the afternoon. As soon as he stopped praying, it began to pour.

In the blistering heat of summer, he and Eleazar went to swim in a nearby lake. Eleazar was ahead of him and almost up to his thighs by the time Yehuda walked into the water. But it wasn't *into*, it was *onto*. To his great astonishment, he was walking on the surface, sinking with each step just an inch or so into the transparent water, as though it had become an expanse of rubber (unknown in the West) stretched out from shore to shore. As he walked, he felt the spray soaking his calves and thighs. It was exhilarating. He hadn't felt this kind of delight since he was a young child. When he got to the middle of the lake, he turned around and waved to Eleazar with a loud halloo.

Most of these forays into the unusual were exciting. They were also seductive. Both men could see how even a meditator who had devoted his life to growing beyond the ego could let supernormal powers go to his head. Ironically, after many years of watching the ego deflate under their intense scrutiny, they had now come to a place where self-aggrandizement, even megalomania, was a real danger. The temptation was no different in kind from the way a worldly man might be tempted by wine. But since these powers were not in their conscious control, they couldn't be summoned or dismissed. The sensible thing to do, as Bodhananda had advised them, was to enjoy them when they appeared and to kiss them goodbye as they left. When supernormal experiences weren't cultivated, Bodhananda said, they usually began to stop after a year or so.

By the beginning of the sixteenth year, most of the powers had fallen away. The only two that kept arising from time to time were the power to see into the past and future and the power to read other people's minds. Bodhananda told them that these were called *trikalajñata* and *para citta adi abhijñata* in the scriptures and that they were the most seductive of all the powers, since they could apparently be used for the benefit of others. The ego was quick to pounce on a desire that masqueraded as generosity or compassion, and many well-intentioned men had found them-selves pulled back into the world of suffering because they thought they knew what was good for other people. They began by trying to control the world for its own benefit and ended by having the ego grow back to consume them.

Eleazar and Yehuda were pleased with their prog-ress, though they realized how far they were from the radiant simplicity of Bodhananda, who had disap-peared into the ordinary as if the world was exactly what it seemed to be, and whose activities consisted of washing clothes, shopping for food, cooking and eat-ing, walking through the countryside, chatting with the villagers, and occasionally playing a game of back-gammon in the evening with the tailor or the shoe-maker. There was nothing unusual about him but his openness of heart. Thoughts that might cause anger, hurt, or sorrow rarely arose in his mind, and when they did, he simply didn't believe them; thus they had no power over him. This absence of suffering, rather than separating him from human experience, made him seem entirely human: the original pattern, the real thing. Eleazar and Yehuda, on the other hand, still occasionally experienced closed-heartedness, anger, or sorrow. They had learned how to let these emotions come and go without judgment and without getting caught up for long in the mental dramas the emotions produce. Their minds had reached, if not a permanent Sabbath, at least a Sabbath that arced out over most of time and space. And they were determined to follow their path to the end, wherever it took them and whatever hardships it might entail. They had made a promise to themselves, and keeping that promise was like the law's first and great commandment, which includes all the others.

3.

When the star appeared in the sky, the two men knew that it was time to go home. It came to them in full daylight, flashing its blue-silver rays a few hundred feet over their heads, darting forward, then back, like a puppy inviting them to play. Sometimes it would vanish after a few minutes, leaving them to search for it like someone who has just awoken from an urgent, unrememberable dream.

There was to be a birth; that much was clear. Who was to be born they didn't know. They knew only that they were being called upon to witness. It would be a great joy for many people, this birth, and they had to be there with gifts to honor the child's arrival. The most manageable gifts, they decided, would be gold coins and precious resins, perhaps myrrh and frankincense from Arabia, which they could buy at the spice merchant's booth in the Cochin bazaar. If the child's parents were rich, these gifts would be commensurate with their dignity. If they were poor, the gifts would support them for many years to come. One of Hillel's sayings had been "The more possessions, the more anxiety," and they considered whether such a splendid offering might not be a hindrance rather than a help. In the end they decided to go ahead with their choice.

Their goodbye to Bodhananda was brief and heartfelt. There was no need to express their profound gratitude, but they expressed it anyway. Bodhananda gave them his blessing, though that too was unnecessary. "Don't forget," he told them, "that any wisdom you have acquired is like soap. You use the soap to wash off the grime, but then you need to wash off the soap."

It was the beginning of June. The distance from Cochin to Jerusalem was about three thousand miles, and the journey took almost seven months. They went by way of Indraprastha, Barbarikon, Taxila, Bactra, Merv, Rhagae, Ecbatana, Ctesiphon, Palmyra, and Damascus, traveling on camelback, joining caravans at the principal gathering points on the Silk Road. All along the way, the star glided before them, three or four hundred feet over their heads, invisible to any eyes but theirs. It stopped at night when they camped, and in the morning it began to move again, ambling along at the caravan's leisurely pace. When they got to Jerusalem, they left the caravan and went on by themselves.

The star came to a final stop directly above a small stable in Bethlehem. It was twilight. A thin covering of snow lay on the ground.

The two men took off their knapsacks, in which, besides the gifts, there were a few loaves of bread, two flasks of Syrian wine, and some winter pears. Then they knocked on the stable door.

A male voice invited them to come in, and they entered. In two stalls on the right side, an ox and a donkey stood watching them. On the left, a very young woman cradled an infant in swaddling clothes. A man stood beside her. In front, between the couple and a shallow stone trough, lay two jars of clotted milk, three squares of butter, and a large cheese, spread out on a woolen mat. The two men made a brief, courteous bow to Yosef (they knew his name without asking) and then to Maryam. When Yosef asked why they had come, Eleazar said, in an Aramaic tinged with a slight Tamil accent, that they had traveled here from the other side of the earth, far to the east, following a star. Then they laid the gifts before Yosef and Maryam, who stared in wonder at the precious objects. Yosef thanked them and asked what the gentlemen wanted. Yehuda said that they wanted nothing at all, but if they could sit with him and his family for a while in silence it would be a great honor. Yosef said that the honor was all his and his wife's.

Since they had Yosef's permission, there was no offense in staring. They looked at him first. They could see what had happened nine months before, the anger and sense of betrayal transformed overnight into a forgiveness so complete that there was no need for it. Both men were filled with inexpressible admiration. They also saw that he had another twenty years of life ahead of him. He would have four sons of his own with Maryam—Yaakov, Yosef, Yehuda, and

Shimon—and two daughters—Sarah and Ruth. He would love them all, but Maryam's firstborn, Yeshua, would be the apple of his eye. As Eleazar and Yehuda looked at Yosef, they saw him teaching the boy to read the holy tongue and memorize the books—Isaiah and Psalms—that would fill his mind with the stirring cadences of Hebrew verse. They saw him showing the young man what integrity looked like in the workshop, marketplace, and home, so that the word *abba*[*] would become for him a symbol for everything upright and generous and fair. Then they saw the family standing around Yosef's dead body, weeping—Maryam and the children, down to the thirteen-year-old Ruth—and saw how devastated Yeshua was and how he would enter a decade of confusion and despair that would end, joyfully, with his baptism.

Then they turned their attention to Maryam. She was looking into the eyes of the infant in her arms. Her expression was the most beautiful thing the two men had ever seen—pure love, which poured down onto the child like the first light of Creation, before sunlight and starlight ever were born. This moment, the two men thought, was blessedness itself. They saw how many

---

[*] Aramaic for "father."

moments like it there would be in the young woman's life, both with Yeshua and with the other six children, and they saw also that the love inside her would nourish her even in the years of heartbreak. They saw the double blow of grief that would come twenty years later, and their hearts went out to her: first the death of Yosef, then Yeshua's years of estrangement, and how even his great transformation would not return him to her as a son. They saw how the rumors of his teachings and healings would frighten her. Here she was now, in one of their visions, which seemed as real as the present scene, at the age of forty-four, with her other sons, traveling the twenty miles from Nazareth in order to seize Yeshua and take him into their safe-keeping, all of them convinced that he had gone out of his mind. And now she was walking away from the house in Capernaum, after Yeshua refused to admit her. Yaakov would put his arm around his mother's waist to steady her as they walked away.

When they turned to the child, a great joy rose through their bodies and made their faces glow with excitement. It didn't have to do with the present moment. How different can one hours-old infant be from any other? This red-faced, squirmy little thing, who had just completed one long journey and was setting out on another, was every child, since every child contained within it the sum of all human possibilities. They felt a fleeting wish to experience the scene as Bodhananda would experience it, without seeing into past and future, completely absorbed in this little family as they were now, the essence of the human condition, man and woman and child—the man standing in the background as provider and protector, with an unshakable integrity and a husbandly, fatherly love spread over his family like a canopy; the woman pouring herself out in a selfless, all-consuming, joyous generosity; and the child receiving it with the openness and surrender of the don't-know mind.

But they couldn't dismiss their supernormal power. They would have to endure it, to honor it, until they arrived at the 360° point, if in fact they ever became mature enough to complete the circle.

And now they were shown who the child would grow up to be. (Though the scenes were in the future, they appeared to the two men as a past.)

In the first one, Yeshua was thirty years old. He was standing on a bank of the Jordan, where the prophet Yoḥanan was preaching a baptism for the forgiveness of sins. Yeshua was still oppressed by grief at the death of his father and by a crushing sense of helplessness and confusion. It was not that he had committed any particular sins—he was, like Yosef, meticulous in his adherence to the law—but he felt an agonizing separation from God. Hundreds of people had come there from all over Judea and Galilee. Yoḥanan had wild hair and wild eyes, and he was clothed in camel skin, with a belt of animal hide around his waist. He spoke with a hypnotic urgency and passion. There were immersions, cheers, groans, sobs. Yeshua waded into the river with the others. They confessed their sins, and then, under Yoḥanan's hands, immersed themselves into the swirling waters. As Yeshua surfaced, his heart opened, and by the time he had walked, dripping, onto the shore, he knew that the kingdom of God had already come. He had returned to his heavenly father. He had been dead and was alive again; had been lost and was found.

The second scene was a series that extended over several days and took place in the wilderness of Judea. Yeshua had been studying with Yoḥanan for three months, and the Baptizer had suggested a forty-day retreat as a further purification. Yeshua had made camp five miles to the southwest of Qumran. The schedule obliged him to sleep for just four hours a night; the rest of the day was to be spent in prayer. The nights were extremely cold. He would lie awake shivering, watching the shadow of the moon on the cliffs as the bats swooped down to feed on insects attracted by the firelight. Sometimes his shivering would be so intense that he couldn't fall asleep, until finally exhaustion triumphed over frigidity.

During the days, he would pray without interruption as he sat, stood, or walked. The wilderness was mostly red rock, with a few scattered mountain springs where sparse vegetation sprang up—mint, willows, and reeds. He would hollow out a grass blade for a straw, then lie down on his belly, dip the straw into the moist ground, and drink. As he walked in the valleys, he would come across small herds of wild goats or onagers; a leopard would sometimes observe him as it lay perched on the branch of an acacia tree, or a jackal would lope briskly across his path.

The two men saw him praying with great fervor. There was a strenuous quality to his prayer, as though, like their ancestor Yaakov, he were wrestling with an angel who had the ferocity of a demon, and he wouldn't let it go until it blessed him. It was the angel of pride, who was all too familiar to each of the men. In the aftermath of a spiritual opening, there was always a rush of exaltation, and they would feel as though they were looking down on humanity from a great height—enlightened beings far above the petty concerns of ordinary, deluded, suffering mortals. The exaltation was genuine, but the prideful thoughts that clustered around it were extra and led to nothing but separation. Yeshua struggled against such thoughts for days, his mind like a roiled pool that has filled with particles from the muddy depths.

Next, Eleazar and Yehuda saw him teaching in Capernaum. He was surrounded by his disciples, and the two men were amazed to see that some of the disciples were women. Yeshua's Aramaic was an instrument of great beauty—elegant, poetic, concise, witty, profound, yet accessible even to the simple fishermen and farmers who sat around him, entranced by what he was saying. He was talking about the kingdom of God. It was the most precious thing in the world, he said, like a pearl of great price, like a treasure buried in a field. Yet it was not something distant from any of them, and it didn't belong to a future. You could watch for the Messiah for thousands of years, he said, and the Messiah would never come. He never *could* come as an outer reality. There would always be people who would say "This is the one" or "That is the one," and they would always be mistaken. The kingdom of God never exists out there, to be seen by physical eyes; it is always here, present, within us. Each of us has to find it for himself, like the pearl or the treasure in the field. And when it is found, the peace inside us becomes an outer peace as well. When we find the kingdom of God in our heart, we can see that it is already spread out over the earth, though very few can see it. We have to become as innocent and trusting as little children in order to enter it. And once we do, it doesn't matter what happens to us on the outside. Illness, poverty, rejection—none of this can trouble us. It all appears as God's unfathomable grace.

They could see the rapture and puzzlement on the faces of the people listening to him. Even his disciples struggled to understand it. This was a teaching unlike anything they had ever heard. For hundreds of years, Jews had been expecting the outer world to change. The prophets had sung their ecstatic, impossible visions of a future, and that was what everyone was looking for. They were looking in the wrong direction, and this mistake would keep them trapped in an endless cycle of hope and disappointment. Yeshua's teaching was the end of the cycle. It was the way out, though it was a difficult way. The two men could feel Hillel's great question reverberate in the air: "If not now, when?"

Yeshua was seeing the whole world through the lens of that profound, urgent, unassimilable question.

To say that he was a brilliant teacher was an understatement. To say that he was a prophet was inaccurate as well, since his mind was clearer and more concept-free than the mind of any prophet had been. What a joy, what a privilege, to see the man this infant would grow up to become! Though they could feel all around him a riveting, magnetic quality of attraction, he looked delicate rather than powerful: shorter than his stepfather, with curly dark-brown hair and beard, his features rather feminine, his nose gracefully arched, his eyes dark brown and brilliant. When his face was in repose and he looked down at the ground, waiting for words to come, his lips showed the traces of a smile.

The final scene took place in Jerusalem. It was right before Passover, and the Romans had made preparations to forestall disorder: a heavily armed cohort on the roof of the portico of the Temple. Below, in the courtyard, Yeshua was teaching. The crowd milled around him, hundreds of pilgrims from all over the land, and his eloquence was stirring them to passion. "The kingdom is coming!" one would say to another. "The kingdom of heaven is coming!" "The Messiah has come!"

"We will drive out the invaders!" "The Messiah! He is here! He has come at last!" As the crowd began to simmer, then boil over with excitement, the soldiers marched down from the roof to disperse them with shouts and spears. Some people in the crowd called out in anger that the priests must have had something to do with this. The soldiers seized Yeshua and marched him away. All the disciples fled.

The captain of the guard brought him to the procurator, a tall, thin man with a bald head and the eyes of a pig. He ordered that the Jew be bound and scourged, then crucified as a rebel and a traitor to Tiberius Caesar. The captain took him outside and flogged him with leather straps fitted with jagged metal spikes until the blood gushed from his wounds. Then they dragged him to the place of execution and pounded heavy iron nails into his hands and feet, impaling him on a wooden cross along with other brigands and insurrectionaries. He hung there for hours, groaning, weak from the loss of blood, struggling against asphyxiation. Flies gathered on his wounds and crawled into his eyes and nose. Finally, a soldier, taking pity on him, killed him with a spear-thrust in his side. His last words, spoken in a gasp, were a quotation from the Psalms:

בְּיָדְךָ אַפְקִיד רוּחִי (B'yadkhá afqíd ruḥí), Into Thy hand I commit my spirit. His body was taken down, thrown into a pit, and quickly buried under the corpses of the crucified.

Eleazar and Yehuda were appalled, yet at the same time overwhelmed with admiration. The tears that rose to their eyes weren't tears of sorrow but rather tears of love for this man, who had faced—who would face—so cruel a death with such dignity, and amid all that excruciating pain had surrendered—would surrender—himself to God from the depths of a peaceful heart. For a fleeting moment a why arose in their minds, but immediately they recognized that this was the wrong question and could only lead to confusion. The lesson, as always, was not in the unknowable why but in the evident what.

But these hours of agony lay in the distant future. Now, in the stable, on this cold winter day, in the deepening twilight, amid the smell of manure and straw, there was only joy. The baby yawned, bunching his hands into tiny fists. Maryam looked up into Yosef's eyes, and they smiled at each other. The good and the ill of any possible future lay in their minds like dormant seeds in the soil. God had made everything beautiful in its own way, in its own time, even what at first seemed appalling. But salvation, which was another name for freedom, would not come later. It could only come now. It had already come, and it was here for everyone, always.

The two men got up and said their goodbyes, then bowed to Maryam and to Yosef. Yehuda was the first to walk out onto the snow-covered ground. Eleazar followed, closing the door gently behind him.

Interlude

I T WAS THE EVANGELIST MATTHEW who added wise men to the Nativity story. His word for them is μάγοι *(magoi),* which turned into our "magi" and can also be translated as "astrologers" or "sorcerers." Men who had been following a secret, itinerant star for three thousand miles might easily be perceived as astrologers. And to be called sorcerers, they wouldn't need to possess psychic powers; even someone with strong spiritual insight might be perceived that way by ignorant, superstitious people.

As for "wise men": that's a concept that calls for some investigation. Wise people don't see themselves as wise; they can't, because they have freed themselves from opposites. "We all have equal wisdom," writes a very wise woman of my acquaintance. "It's equally distributed. No one is wiser than anyone else. The only difference is that some of us believe what we think, and some of us have learned to question the thoughts that separate us from our inborn wisdom."

Another way of putting this: "Your original wisdom is like the full moon," my old Zen Master once said. "Sometimes clouds come and cover it, but the moon is always behind them. When the clouds go away, the moon shines. So don't worry about reaching that wisdom: it is always there. When thinking comes, behind it is original mind. When thinking goes, there is only original mind in the clear sky. You must not be attached to the coming or the going." This explanation is easy to understand, but not so easy to put into practice. It may take years. It may take a lifetime.

Today, as I meditated on what more I could say about my wise men, I found myself imagining a crèche patterned on the characters in this book. The young family are in the center, halo-free of course. The ox and the donkey peer out at them, affectionately, from their stalls. To the left, as we look on, the three shepherds kneel, hands folded in prayer. To the right stand the two wise men, dressed in simple but elegant reddish-brown robes, with white skullcaps on their heads. There are no angels.

And now, after their long, marveling gaze at Maryam, Yosef, and the baby, the wise men turn their attention to the shepherds. They are deeply moved by the beauty of these three unwashed men in their ragged homespun robes, kneeling on the cold ground without any awareness of its coldness, giving themselves entirely to their act of veneration. The wise men see that the shepherds' gift of clotted ewe's milk, butter, and cheese is equal to their own extravagant gift of gold, frankincense, and myrrh and that the simple reverence of these men is equal to all the wisdom they themselves have acquired during twenty-six years of passionate contemplation. Everyday mind is the Way.

7

The Donkey

Better one shrewd donkey than ten strong horses.

—PROVERBS OF LEMUEL 3:11

IT HAS BEEN QUITE a busy day here in the stable, what with the shepherds coming and then the wise men and the innkeeper popping in and out to see how my mistress is doing, and throughout the day angels from every order of the hierarchy descending to take a peek at the new little visitor. They don't knock or announce themselves; they just fly in through the roof or the walls, without so much as a by-your-leave, and nobody greets or even notices them. When they see me, though, they nod to acknowledge my presence and to let me know that they know I know. Some of them smile, and I have even caught one of them in a wink. The smiles come from the lower orders, of course, the young ones who are working their way up through the ranks. The cherubim with their calf's feet, four wings, and four faces—lion, eagle, ox, and man—are too exalted to greet me, and the ardent seraphim, so huge that they have to compress themselves in order to fit in the stable, never take their focus from the human family, and anyway I can't see their faces, since they cover them with two of their wings, while with two wings they cover their bodies and with two they hover in the air like dragonflies. I don't expect even the slightest gesture of acknowledgment from such august beings. Still, would it be so hard to turn their heads for a moment and give me a quick nod?

Ancient donkey tradition traces our ability to see angels back to the visionary ancestress who belonged, as humans put it, to the Moabite prophet Balaam. We donkeys all know the story, but perhaps you need a reminder. Briefly, then: Balaam was called upon by Balak, king of the Moabites, to curse the children of Israel as they passed through Moab on their way to the Promised Land. Naturally, the Lord forbade him to do that. But Balaam saddled his (quote unquote) donkey anyway, and he rode out with the princes of Moab.

Here comes the important part. An angel holding a drawn sword stood in his path to block him. This happened three times, and each time our ancestress saw the angel, though Balaam didn't, and she responded as any reasonable donkey would respond. The first time, she swerved out of the road and into a field. Balaam beat her with his staff for that. The second time, with a wall on either side of her, she slammed his foot against one wall, and he beat her again. The third time, when there was no way to turn, she simply lay down under him. By now he was so frustrated at her apparent obstinacy that he started beating her savagely.

This is the crisis point of the story. What do you think happened next? Well, our distinguished ancestress opened her mouth and spoke human words. It wasn't that she couldn't speak before. We all can, but we choose not to. It's a matter of discretion. Since we have been brought up to a life of service, we realize that letting humans know of our verbal abilities only muddies distinctions and confuses categories. In short, it doesn't serve.

Anyway, our ancestress spoke out in classical Hebrew and said, מֶה עָשִׂיתִי לְךָ כִּי הִכִּיתַנִי זֶה שָׁלֹשׁ רְגָלִים *(Méh asíti l'khá kí hikitáni zéh shalósh r'galím?)*, "What have I done to make you beat me these three times?" Now the crucial thing to notice here is that Balaam, being a man of insight, was not at all surprised that she had spoken to him. He answered her matter-of-factly, though with a good deal of heat. "You have made a fool of me," he said, etc. And our ancestress, with the deductive power of a true philosopher, said, "Am I not your (quote unquote) donkey? Haven't you ridden me all my life?" (I consider this sentence a particularly poignant statement of her devotion.) "Have I ever done anything like this before?" Since Balaam wasn't a fool, he followed her chain of reasoning until finally his eyes were opened. Upon which he too saw the angel, who told Balaam that if it hadn't been for the visionary female he had been riding, he would have been slain right there on the spot.

I, like all donkeys in the lands of Galilee and Judea, honor this great ancestress for many things, not the least of which is her courage in speaking out under extremely trying circumstances. She was not one to suffer unfair treatment without protesting—and in the most forthright manner. Then there is her power of vision, which has given her descendants permission to be visionaries themselves. I don't know what donkeys are capable of in foreign lands, but in our land even the youngest colt has the innate capacity to see angels—at least the lower orders of them—though not everyone is able to see cherubim and seraphim as the most gifted among us are.

Then there is her exquisite honesty. Who among humans, even under the threat of death, would be willing to speak the truth, exactly as she saw it? When I contemplate her unswerving integrity, the integrity that made her swerve from her master's path, I am deeply moved and honored that she is the founding mother of our glorious visionary tradition. There have been others who have followed in her hoofsteps, but here in the lands of Galilee and Judea, she is an inspiration to us all.

Finally, I would like to point out her refusal to capitulate to authority. This is a most admirable quality, and it is at the core of our character. Some humans call it stubbornness, but it is actually a mode of intelligence. We can't be frightened or forced to do anything that is opposed to our own best interest, however devoted we may be to our master or mistress, and our best interest always turns out to be theirs as well. When we refuse to work, it is because the work is impossible; some human has overbalanced or overburdened us, and we wait patiently until he figures out where he has gone wrong. Or else, for example, it is because he is trying to direct us on a path with unsure footing. Now horses, those proud but subservient creatures who for the most part lack any capacity for critical thinking, will go down whatever path you ask them to, and this can lead to disaster—on a steep mountain trail, for example. It is not that horses are nitwits, but by no stretch of the imagination can they be called intelligent in our donkeyish sense of the word. We are easier to train than they are and more willing to work when it seems reasonable to us, though never willing to proceed on blind faith. "You can command a horse," as the human saying goes, "but with a donkey you have to negotiate."

I sometimes wonder how we got our reputation for stubbornness and stupidity. When one human calls another human a donkey, it is not, ironically enough, a compliment. But humans love servility. Their exemplar of piety is the sheep, that truly brainless animal. And just look at the submissiveness of horses and oxen, not to speak of the creature absurdly called man's best friend, the dog, who can be found in many assimilated households throughout our land. Is there any more fawning, servile creature on the face of the earth? The dog is brought up with an absolute slave mentality, and so indoctrinated is he that he would as soon give up a meal as question even the most nonsensical or degrading of his master's directives. He is entirely without dignity. He will even play the fool for a scrap of food or a caress. Pitiful.

This reputation of ours annoys me, when I bother to think of it at all. Stupid? I'll tell you what stupid is. There is a prophecy here that when the Messiah arrives, he will come riding upon one of us. Most people, and most donkeys for that matter, believe the prophet—if not in a literal, at least in a symbolic, sense. Humble is as humble does. But some of our Hellenized Jews, who have lost touch with their ancestral culture and even with their ancestral tongue, believe that the Messiah will come riding on *two* donkeys. Can you imagine? One man riding on two donkeys at once? I'm not joking! They say this—and I suppose that they picture the man with his right leg thrown over the right flank of one and his left leg over the left flank of the other, if such an awkward posture is even physically possible—because the prophet said, "He will be riding upon a donkey / and upon a colt, the foal of a donkey." These people don't understand the first thing about Hebrew poetry: its most distinctive feature, parallelism, where successive verses state the same concept in two different ways. The donkey *is* the colt. The great man won't be riding astride a donkey *and* a colt but astride a donkey, period. I'll say it again: not two of us but one. It's like the ancient hero Lamech, who "slew a man for wounding him, / and a young man for hurting him." He didn't slay two men; there was only *one* man, twice stated, in formulations that are slightly different. But these Greek-speaking illiterates think that there were two corpses and two donkeys. How asinine, so to speak, can you get?

The other species stereotype, besides stupidity, is loudness, which is a code word for crudeness. Humans aren't the only ones with this prejudice; I have known horses too (usually the mares rather than the stallions) who consider us beneath their dignity. As you'd expect, the only humans who entertain this stereotype are the ones who don't know us. Actually, our brays are quite rare. When we move in a herd, there is rarely a peep from anyone. Only when we're in a state of acute physical distress, or sexually aroused beyond our endurance, or separated for too long from our best friend, will you hear us raise our voices. But, of course, if you ask a young city child, "What does a donkey say?" the answer, sadly, will be "Hee-haw!"

Speaking of best friends, it's been a week now since I've been away from mine, and I'm starting to miss her. We have always been together, ever since we were colts. We live side by side, and we work together as a team, and very good work we do, if I say so myself. I have been separated from her before, once for two weeks, and it has always been stressful. I am not yet at the braying point, but I *am* feeling uneasy. I hope that my mistress will be going home to Nazareth soon, though obviously what has been happening here in Bethlehem must have some sort of unusual significance, what with all the visitors, both human and angelic. Some donkeys have been known to pine away and even die of heartbreak when they are separated from their special friend for too long. This will not happen to me, because I have a very strong character. Also, I am completely devoted to my mistress. I would even undergo this uneasiness for a longer time if that might serve her in some way. But I do miss my friend.

This ox in the stall beside me is a decent stable-mate, as oxen go. He is well-mannered and considerate, and he doesn't snort much. But I would never have an ox as a friend. They are such dull, lumbering oafs. No wonder there is a law against yoking us together for plowing. It would be just too frustrating. All day long they have to stop and ruminate. What could they be thinking about? And why stop and think at all? When you're working, why not just work? We outperform them anyway. Not only are we more efficient, but we eat less, pound for pound, and we learn much more quickly. Ah, the infinite slowness of the ox brain. I sometimes wonder if they even *have* brains, or is there just an expanse of prime steak between those two horns?

Perhaps right now he is ruminating upon all the fuss—the shepherds with their gifts, then the wise men with *their* gifts—though, not being a donkey, he can have no idea how much fuss there has actually been. My master and mistress have no idea either, since all the angelic visitors have been as quiet and unobtrusive as mice. There hasn't been one note of celestial music or one audible rustle of wings. But the visiting has been constant. I have never seen the birth of a human before. It is obviously a very big deal.

I know that my mistress trusts me. After all, I just carried her for six days without a single misstep. Besides, she has known my character ever since the day she came to my master's house. I fell in love with her then, and though I am devoted to them both, if I had to choose I would choose her. She knows how gentle I am and how trustworthy. All of which is to say that I would make an excellent nurse for the child, if she should ever need me in that capacity. I am my lady's handmaid. I would do anything for her. She has only to ask.

Interlude

I FIND IT DELIGHTFULLY TRICKSTERISH OF YOU," a friend of mine wrote in a recent email, "that of all your characters, you've let a donkey who chooses not to speak have the last word." I'm glad my friend was delighted, but if there is a trickster here, it isn't me; it's God, a.k.a. reality. The form of this book is xcc¹dd¹ee¹ee¹dd¹cc¹x, like the glorified sestet of an Italian sonnet, where x is a blank, c stands for an animal, d a group of humans, and e a human protagonist, and the 1 superscript means an interlude. So because the ox came second, the donkey had to come last. This form is implied in the composite Nativity story, where ox rhymes with donkey, shepherds rhyme with wise men, and Mary rhymes with Joseph. I didn't invent the pattern; I merely perceived it. Nor did I invent the silent but speech-capable nature of donkeys; it was already there, waiting to be appropriated, in the wonderful story of Balaam, which every donkey-lover in the world will read with a frisson of recognition.

There are many things you might criticize my little visionary donkey for. She is vain, resentful, intolerant, competitive, racist (or is it speciesist?) … I could go on, and I can find every unpleasant quality in myself—if not now, then at earlier times in my life. But in the end, she is blameless; any blame belongs to me, since I'm the one who made her the way she is. I must confess, though, that I felt a great deal of pleasure in giving her these qualities. After so much soulfulness and surrender on the part of Maryam, Yosef, and the two wise men, her cantankerousness seemed to add just the right amount of pungency to keep things from becoming too sweet, as Nativity stories tend to be. So it seemed only fitting that she should have the last word.

Except that her word is not quite the last one. I still have a few more to add.

Epilogue

THE CELEBRATION OF THE FIRST CHRISTMAS lacked anything we would recognize as festive; there were no "holly, mistletoe, red berries, ivy, turkeys, geese, game, poultry, brawn, meat, pigs, sausages, oysters, pies, puddings, fruit, and punch," no pine, spruce, or fir tree, and (it seems ludicrous even to say this) no Santa Claus. I have nothing against Christmas trees or against Santa, that Disneyfied reincarnation of Odin, the one-eyed, white-bearded god who rides across the yuletide heavens on his eight-legged steed, Sleipnir, bringing gifts to young and old, shouting the Old Norse equivalent of "Ho, ho, ho!" But, social merriment aside, the essence of Christmas must have been present at the first Christmas, in a ramshackle barn with two young people whose love had overcome the most difficult of obstacles.

I hope that your imagination of the Nativity scene has become more vivid now after reading my story.

But it's not enough to watch the scene from the outside. "If Christ's birth doesn't happen in me, how can it help me?" said Meister Eckhart in one of the epigraphs at the beginning of my story. "Everything depends on that."

What did he mean by "Christ's birth in me"? It's another way of saying "the coming of the Messiah inside me"—that is, the coming of an immovable inner peace that will last for a thousand, a million years. *Peace on earth, good will to men*: if that peace doesn't happen inside me, how can I expect to see it in the world outside, which is a reflection of the perceiving mind? Allowing it to arise—or, more accurately, clearing away the obstacles to its natural arising—is the great mission that has been given to us all. When we find peace on earth, good will toward humans and toward every sentient being happens by itself.

Appendix: The Two Infancy Narratives

From Luke's story:

Now the angel Gabriel was sent by God to a city in Galilee called Nazareth, to a virgin engaged in marriage to a man descended from King David whose name was Joseph, and the virgin's name was Mary. The angel came to her and said, "Greetings, favored one; the Lord is with you." She was greatly troubled by his words and wondered what such a greeting could mean. And the angel said to her, "Do not be afraid, Mary, for you have found favor with God. You will conceive in your womb and give birth to a son, and you will name him Jesus. He will be great and will be called the Son of the Most High. And the Lord God will give him the throne of his forefather David,

184 • APPENDIX: THE TWO INFANCY NARRATIVES

and he will reign over the people of Israel forever, and his kingdom will never end."

Then Mary said to the angel, "How can this be, since I have not had sex with a man?"

The angel answered, "The Holy Spirit will come upon you, and the power of the Most High will overshadow you. Therefore the child to be born will be holy, the Son of God. For with God nothing is impossible."

Mary said, "I am the handmaid of the Lord. Let it happen to me as you have said." And the angel left her.

At that time, a decree went out from Caesar Augustus that a census should be taken through the whole world. (This was the first census under Quirinius as governor of Syria.) So everyone went to be registered in his own city. Joseph traveled from the city of Nazareth in Galilee to Judea, to the city of David, which is called Bethlehem, because he was a descendant of David, to be registered with Mary, who was with child. And while they were there, the time came for her to be delivered, and she gave birth to her firstborn son. And she wrapped him in swaddling clothes and laid him in a manger, because there was no room for them at the inn.

There were shepherds out in a field nearby, keeping watch over their flock by night. And an angel appeared to them, and the glory of the Lord shone all around them, and they were very afraid. Then the angel said to them, "Do not be afraid. For I bring you good news that will bring a great joy to all the people. Today, in the city of David, a savior has been born for you, who is the lord Messiah. And this is how you will recognize him: You will find an infant, wrapped in swaddling clothes, lying in a manger."

Suddenly with the angel there was a multitude of the heavenly host praising God and saying, "Glory to God in the highest heavens, and on earth peace, good will toward men."

When the angels had left them and gone back to heaven, the shepherds said to one another: "Let us go to Bethlehem and see this thing that the Lord has announced to us." So they hurried there and found Mary and Joseph with the infant, who was lying in a manger. And after they had seen the child, they told everyone the message they had been given about him. All who heard it were astonished at what the shepherds told them. And Mary observed all these things carefully and pondered them in her heart. The shepherds returned to their flock, glorifying God and praising Him for all the things they had seen and heard, which happened just as they had been told.

From Matthew's story:

This is how the birth of Jesus came about. His mother, Mary, had been engaged in marriage to Joseph, but before they had come together, she was found to be with child through the Holy Spirit. Her husband, Joseph, was a righteous man and was unwilling to expose her to public disgrace, so he decided to divorce her in private. But as he was considering this, an angel appeared to him in a dream and said, "Joseph, son of David, do not be afraid to take Mary as your wife, for the child has been conceived in her through the Holy Spirit. She will give birth to a son, and you shall name him Jesus, for he will save his people from their sins." When Joseph awoke from his sleep, he did as the angel had commanded him, and he married her and took her home with him. But he didn't have sex with her until after she had given birth to a son, and he named the child Jesus.

Now after Jesus was born in Bethlehem, wise men from the East came to Jerusalem and asked, "Where is the child who has been born king of the Jews? We saw his star in the East, and we have come to worship him." (The star that they had seen in the East had gone before them, until it stood over the place where the child was. When they had seen the star, they had rejoiced with very great joy.) And when they entered the house, they saw the child with Mary, his mother, and they bowed down and worshiped him. And they opened their treasure boxes and brought out gifts for him: gold, frankincense, and myrrh. Then they went back to their own country.

Notes and References

All translations are mine unless otherwise indicated.

xiii, *Christ's birth is always happening*: *Meister Eckhart: A Modern Translation*, trans. Raymond Bernard Blakney, New York: Harper and Row, 1941, 95 (translation slightly modified).

xiii, *At the Passover seder*: I have been unable to trace the source of this story. I may have heard it from my old friend the late Rabbi Zalman Schachter.

1, *the Nativity story*: Neither Matthew's story nor Luke's, which contradict each other in many essential details, has any historical basis, and there is no historical corroboration of details such as the Roman census or the so-called Massacre of the Innocents.

2, *given to us all*: Isa. 9:6.

3, *the phrase "son of God"*: Here are the facts according to the excellent scholar E. P. Sanders: "Because of the birth narratives in Matthew and Luke, modern readers often think that 'Son of God' meant 'a male conceived in the absence of human semen' or even 'a male half human and half divine, produced when God fertilized a human ovum without semen.' . . . No ancient Jew, to our knowledge, used 'Son of God' in such a crudely literal sense. The common Jewish use was generic: all Jews were 'Sons of God' (the masculine in this case included females). The use of the singular 'Son of God' to refer to a specific person would be surprising, but it would not make the hearer think of unnatural modes of conception and of a hybrid offspring . . . The title would imply special

standing before God and an unusual power to accomplish good."
The Historical Figure of Jesus, New York: Penguin Books, 1995, 243.

3, *Be fruitful and multiply*: Gen. 1:28.

4, *Søren Kierkegaard astutely pointed out*: *Frygt og Bæven*, Copenhagen: Reitzel, 1895, 74.

9, *Jove nods to Jove from behind each of us*: "The Over-Soul" in *Essays, First Series*, Boston: Houghton, Mifflin and Company, 1883, 261.

15, *a bray that was like a pump gone dry*: I have pilfered this simile from Elizabeth Bishop's wonderful poem "Manuelzinho" in *Questions of Travel*, New York: Farrar, Straus and Giroux, 1965, 17.

17, *no room for them at the inn*: "The Greek word *kataluma* may be translated as either 'inn' or 'guestroom,' and some scholars have speculated that Joseph and Mary may have sought to stay with relatives, rather than at an inn, only to find the house full, whereupon they resorted to the shelter of a room with a manger." (https://en.wikipedia.org/wiki/Nativity_of_Jesus) See Raymond E. Brown, *The Birth of the Messiah*, New Haven: Yale University Press, 1999, 401.

18, *as the Bhagavad Gita helpfully points out*: *Bhagavad Gita*, trans. Stephen Mitchell, New York: Harmony Books, 2000, 83.

22, *that is forbidden by law*: Deut. 22:10.

22, *neither have cloven hoofs nor chew the cud*: Lev. 11:3.

27, *Joy took the shape of my body*: Jules Supervielle, "Le bœuf et l'âne de la crèche" in *L'enfant de la haute mer*, Paris: Gallimard, 1931, 43.

27, *wolves will dwell in peace with lambs*: Isa. 11:6–7.

30, *swords have been transformed*: Isa. 2:4.

36, *On earth peace toward men of good will*: Or, more literally, "among men of [his] good pleasure." This is the preferred reading of *The Greek New Testament*, 3rd ed., Stuttgart: United Bible Societies, 1983, 207, though many ancient manuscripts reflect the reading "good will toward men." (There is a one-letter difference in the Greek texts: εὐδοκίας / εὐδοκία.) In the accompanying textual commentary, Bruce M. Metzger writes: "The genitive case, which is the more difficult reading, is supported by the oldest representatives of the Alexandrian and the Western groups of witnesses." *A Textual Commentary on the Greek New Testament*, Stuttgart: United Bible Societies, 1975, 133.

37, *along with the lambs*: Isa. 65:25.

38, *the angels who appeared to our father Abraham*: Gen. 18:1–15.

46, *a still, small voice*: 1 Kings 19:12.

47, *Every angel is terrifying*: Rainer Maria Rilke, *Duineser Elegien*, Leipzig: Insel-Verlag, 1923, 7. See *The Selected Poetry of Rainer Maria Rilke*, ed. and trans. Stephen Mitchell, New York: Random House, 1982, 151.

51, *doing laundry at the rocky cistern*: In the back of my mind as I wrote this was the stanza from Yeats's poem "The Mother of God" that begins "Had I not found content among the shows ..."

52, *singing from place to place*: Here I was thinking of Sarah Pierpont (1710–1758), the wife of the Calvinist theologian Jonathan Edwards. Edwards wrote of her: "They say there is a young lady in [New-Haven] who is loved of that Great Being, who made and rules the world, and that there are certain seasons in which this Great Being, in some way or other invisible, comes to her and fills her mind with exceeding sweet delight; and that she hardly cares for any thing except to meditate on Him—that she expects after a while to be received up where He is, to be raised up out of the world and caught up into heaven; being assured that He loves her too well to let her remain at a distance from him always. There she is to dwell with Him, and to be ravished with His love and delight forever. Therefore, if you present all the world before her, with the richest of its treasures, she disregards it and cares not for it, and is unmindful of any pain or affliction. She has a strange sweetness in her mind, and singular purity in her affections; is most just and conscientious in all her conduct; and you could not persuade her to do anything wrong or sinful, if you would give her all the world, lest she should offend this Great Being. She is of a wonderful sweetness, calmness, and universal benevolence of mind; especially after this Great God has manifested himself to her mind. She will sometimes go about from place to place, singing sweetly; and seems to be always full of joy and pleasure; and no one knows for what. She loves to be alone, walking in the fields and groves, and seems to have some one invisible always conversing with her." *The Works of Jonathan Edwards, A.M.*, vol. 1, London: William Ball, 1839, lxxxi–lxxxii.

53, *one flesh*: Gen. 2:24.

54, *Let him kiss me with the kisses of his mouth*: Song 1:1.

56, *the angel is pure intelligence*: Stephen Mitchell, *Meetings with the Archangel*, New York: HarperCollins, 1998, 125–27, 129.

56, *The ultimate human felicity*: Thomas Aquinas, *Summa Contra Gentiles*, Book 3: Providence, Q. 50.

57, *heaven in a wild flower*: William Blake, "Auguries of Innocence" in *The Complete Poetry and Prose of William Blake*, ed. David V. Erdman, Berkeley and Los Angeles: University of California Press, 1982, 490.

58, *with tilted brow dismisses*: "Der Engel," in Rainer Maria Rilke, *Neue Gedichte*, Leipzig: Insel Verlag, 1907, 42. My translation first appeared in *Meetings with the Archangel*, 137.

61, *tinkling feet*: "Moreover the Lord says, 'Because the daughters of Zion are haughty, and walk with outstretched necks and wanton eyes, walking and mincing as they go, and making a tinkling with their feet," Isa. 3:16.

62, *All who are led by the spirit of God*: Rom. 8:14.

62, *You are my son*: Ps. 2:7.

64, *seven hundred wives and three hundred concubines*: 1 Kings 11:3.

65, *had warned the people about kings*: 1 Sam. 8:11–18.

65, *scatter the great in their arrogance*: Luke 1:51–53.

66, *the nations would beat their swords into plowshares:* Isa. 2:4.

67, *out of Zion the law*: Isa. 2:3.

67, *the crooked be made straight*: Isa. 40:4–5.

68, *like Abraham and Job*: Gen. 25:8, Job 42:17.

68, *like David's cup*: Ps. 23:5.

70, *like the prophets Noah and Job*: Gen. 6:9 ("Noah was a righteous man, blameless [or: perfect] among the people of his time"), Job 1:1 ("that man was perfect and upright"), 1:8, 2:3.

70, *leave their fathers and mothers*: Gen. 2:24.

70, *Having children is a commandment*: Gen. 1:28.

73, *turns out to be God*: According to later Jewish tradition, it was an angel that Jacob wrestled with. But in the biblical text (Gen. 32:25), the Hebrew word, אִישׁ *('ish)*, which usually means "man," means "supernatural being" (the word has the same meaning in the first chapter of Zechariah), and the being himself says, in the self-referential third person: "You have struggled with God." Besides, Jacob clearly states the reason he named the place Penuel (The Face of God): "I saw God face to face, yet my life was spared," Gen. 32:28, 30.

74–75, *Then one of the seraphim*: Isa. 6:1–8.

77, *Behold, the young woman shall conceive*: Isa. 7:14. The Hebrew word עַלְמָה *(almah)* means "a young woman of marriageable age"; there is another word for "virgin": בְּתוּלָה *(b'tulah)*. (In Prov. 30:19, "the way of a man with an *almah*" probably refers to the sexual act, one of the four phenomena that the writer sees as a cause for great wonder.)

82, *Whither thou goest, I will go*: Ruth 1:16.

82, *to love God with all her heart*: Deut. 6:5.

83, *the lame man leaps like a deer*: Isa. 35:6.

84, *I am the handmaid of the Lord*: Luke 1:38, 46–48.

87, *After the final no*: "The Well Dressed Man with a Beard" in Wallace Stevens, *Parts of a World*, New York: Alfred A. Knopf, 1942, 118.

90, *This is the way of the adulteress*: Prov. 30:20.

90, *I have seen you commit adultery*: Jer. 13:27, 2:20.

91, *The Lord is my shepherd*: Ps. 23:1.

94, *the excellent woman of Proverbs*: Prov. 31:10.

95, *nearer than breath, than heartbeat*: Stephen Mitchell, *The Enlightened Heart: An Anthology of Sacred Poetry*, New York: Harper & Row, 1989, 4.

95, *left with nothing but gratitude and laughter*: Byron Katie, *Loving What Is*, New York: Harmony Books, 2002, 33.

95, *the way light rushes*: Dante, *Purgatorio*, xv, 69.

96, *he wanted no more for himself*: Cf. Dante, *Paradiso*, iii, 70–75.

97, *the First Commandment*: Ex. 20:3.

98, *Who can understand his errors?*: Ps. 19:12–13.

98, *had patronized a harlot*: Gen. 38:15–18.

100, *The law of the Lord is perfect*: Ps. 19:7.

101, *In them is a path for the sun*: Ps. 19:4–6.

101, *Then I will be blameless*: Ps. 19:13.

102, *May the words of my mouth*: Ps. 19:14.

102, *Whoever looks carefully*: James 1:25.

103, *What good is it, my brothers*: James 2:14–17.

104, *before the rabbis realized*: The punishment of being stoned to death hadn't been invoked by a Jewish court for many centuries; the rabbis had so modified it—had so hedged it around with many restrictions—that it had been defined out of existence. The law (Talmud Sanh. 40b, 41a, a much later text, which may, however, reflect the legal situation at the time of Jesus) stated that a woman could be convicted of adultery only if there were two unimpeachable eyewitnesses to the act; the witnesses had to warn her that she was about to commit a capital offense; she had to acknowledge the warning and commit the sin anyway, having sexual intercourse in plain sight of them; then the witnesses had to be meticulously cross-examined by a panel of judges, separately, neither one being able to hear the testimony of the other; and if there was even the most trivial discrepancy between the two accounts, the case had to be dismissed. It was almost unheard-of for a Jewish court to condemn anyone to death, even for murder. "A court that invokes the death penalty even once in seven years," the rabbis said, "is rightly considered murderous." "Once in *seventy* years," said Rabbi Eleazar ben Azariah (first century CE). Mishnah Makk. 7a.

104, *Do not judge your neighbor until you are in his situation*: Mishnah Ab. 2:5.

105, *charm is deceptive*: Prov. 31:30.

106, *The law was unequivocal*: Deut. 22:25–26.

108, *a bastard was not to enter the congregation of the Lord*: Deut. 3:2.

108, *stood among the myrtle trees*: Zech. 1:7ff. (The second year of Darius was 520 BCE.)

108, *the sons of God had seen*: Gen. 6:2, 4.

109, *twelve fingers and toes*: This tradition about the *nephilim* is based on 2 Sam. 21:20, which mentions a Philistine giant, "a huge man with six fingers on each hand and six toes on each foot—twenty-four in all. He was descended from the giants."

110, *Go now, marry a whore*: Hos. 1:2.

111, *even if she only burned a meal*: Talmud Git. 90a.

114, *You are my son*: Ps. 2:7.

115, *It is God who brings messages in dreams*: Gen. 31:24.

115, *angels always deliver their messages in waking time*: Gen. 16:7–12, 18:1–15 (Yahweh, as one of the three "[supernatural] beings," counts as an angel here), 21:17–18, 22:11–12, and so on.

120, *Have mercy upon me, O God*: Ps. 51:1ff.

120, *Wash me*: Ps. 51:7–8, 11.

122, *the words of his mouth*: Cf. Ps. 19:14.

123, *ascend the mountain of the Lord*: Ps. 24:3–4, 7.

124, *delight in the law of the Lord*: Ps. 1:2.

124, *he would not sleep with her until*: Matt. 1:25.

125, *Arise, my beloved*: Song 2:10–13.

126, *Joseph, was a righteous man*: Matt. 1:19–21, 24–25.

127, *green-eyed monster*: Shakespeare, *Othello*, 3.3.171.

127, *one of the three "most pathetic of human compositions"*: *The Tragedies of William Shakespeare*, London: Henry Froude, Oxford University Press, 1912, part 9, 6. (The other two are "Plato's records of the last scenes of the career of Socrates and Walton's *Life of George Herbert*.")

127, *the noblest man of man's making*: Ibid.

128, *my noble Moor*: *Othello*, 3.4.16–18.

129, *However men try to reach Me*: *Bhagavad Gita*, trans. Stephen Mitchell, 73.

131, *there were three of them*: "Since the Evangelist does not say how many of them there were, it is better not to know than to recklessly affirm as certain what is doubtful. Because St. Matthew says that they brought gold, frankincense, & myrrh, the Papists imagine that there were three of them; but they go too far & show how childish their judgment is. For the Evangelist does not mean that each one presented a separate gift, but that they presented these three things in common ... But the most ridiculous thing the Papists have done is to dream these wise men into kings." *Commentaires de Iean Calvin sur la Concordance ou Harmonie, composee des Trois Euangelistes, assavoir sainct Mattieu, sainct Marc, & sainct Luc*, Genève: Michel Blanchier, 1563, 50.

131, *not only wise men but kings*: They weren't kings until 420 years after Matthew's Gospel was written, when a Greek manuscript crowned them and gave them the marvelous names Gaspar, Melchior, and Balthasar.

132, *Hillel*: Hillel the Elder (110 BCE–10 CE), sage, scholar, and jurist. As a young man, while devoting himself to studying the Torah, he also worked as a woodcutter.

132, *Whatever is unpleasant to you*: Talmud Shab. 31a.

132–33, *If I am not for myself*: Mishnah Ab. 1:14.

133, *for as long as the earth*: "It was believed that the earliest Jews in India were sailors from King Solomon's time. It has been claimed that following the destruction of the First Temple in the Siege of Jerusalem of 587 BCE, some Jewish exiles came to India … Central to the history of the Cochin Jews was their close relationship with Indian rulers. This was codified on a set of copper plates granting the community special privileges … Indian rulers granted the Jewish leader Joseph Rabban the rank of prince over the Jews of Cochin, giving him the rulership and tax revenue of a pocket principality in Anjuvannam near Cranganore, and rights to seventy-two 'free houses.' The Hindu king gave permission in perpetuity (or, in the more poetic expression of those days, 'as long as the world and moon exist') for Jews to live freely, build synagogues, and own property 'without conditions attached.'" (https://en.wikipedia.org/wiki/Cochin_Jews)

134, *He who does not increase his knowledge*: Mishnah Ab. 1:13.

134, *If I am here*: Talmud Suk. 53a.

134, *whose true name … is* I am: Ex. 3:14.

135, *not to separate themselves from the Jewish community*: Mishnah Ab. 2:5.

135, *forbidden the worship of any god but Himself*: Ex. 20:3.

136, *I am black and beautiful*: Song 1:5.

139, *Where shall wisdom be found*: Job 28:12.

139, *Yet only seekers can find it*: Abu Yazid al-Bistami, in *The Enlightened Mind*, ed. Stephen Mitchell, New York: HarperCollins, 1991, 76.

143, *This path … is like a circle: Dropping Ashes on the Buddha: The Teaching of Zen Master Seung Sahn*, comp. and ed. Stephen Mitchell, New York: Grove Press, 1976, 5–8.

144, *like thirsting for water: Be As You Are: The Teachings of Sri Ramana Maharshi*, ed. David Godman, London: Arkana, 1985, 104.

144, *When your understanding has passed: Bhagavad Gita*, trans. Stephen Mitchell, 55.

145, *naming every plant and animal for the first time*: This passage is based on an exercise in Byron Katie's School for The Work.

146, *There was only the one!*: Cf. Byron Katie, *A Mind at Home with Itself*, San Francisco: HarperOne, 2017, 4.

146, *Emptiness, pure emptiness*: Eccles. 1:1, 3, 11.

147, *has made everything beautiful in its own time*: Eccles. 3:11.

148, *Antigonus of Sokho*: A scholar who flourished during the first half of the third century BCE. His only preserved saying is "Don't be like servants who serve their master in order to receive a reward, but be like servants who serve their master for his sake, not in order to receive a reward. And let the awe of God be upon you." Pirkei Avot i.3.

149, *Honi the Circle-Drawer*: Jewish scholar of the first century BCE. The legend of his praying for rain occurs in the Talmud, Ta'an. 19a.

150, trikalajñata *and* para citta adi abhijñata: *Bhagavata Purana*, 11.15.8–9.

153, *The more possessions, the more anxiety*: Mishnah Ab. 2:8.

155–56, *Yaakov, Yosef, Yehuda, and Shimon*: Mark 6:3.

157, *in order to seize Yeshua*: Mark 3:21.

157, *she was walking away from the house*: Mark 3:31ff.

158, *a baptism for the forgiveness of sins*: Mark 1:4–6.

159, *clothed in camel skin*: Mark 1:6.

159, *Yeshua waded into the river*: Mark 1:9.

159, *He had been dead*: Luke 15:24.

159, *in the wilderness of Judea*: Mark 1:13.

160, *he wouldn't let it go until it blessed him*: Gen. 32:26.

161, *like a pearl of great price, like a treasure buried in a field*: Matt. 13:44–46.

161, *You could watch for the Messiah*: Luke 17:20.

162, *it is always here, present, within us*: Luke 17:21.

162, *it is already spread out over the earth*: Gospel of Thomas, logion 113.

162, *as little children*: Mark 10:15 (= Matt. 18:3).

163, *the Romans had made preparations*: Of another occasion, the historian Josephus writes: "Large crowds had assembled in Jerusalem for the festival of unleavened bread, and a Roman cohort had been stationed on the roof of the portico of the Temple (a body of men in arms always keeps guard at the festivals, to prevent any disorders arising from such large crowds)." Josephus, *The Judean War*, 2.12.1.

164, *All the disciples fled*: Mark 14:50.

165, *Into Thy hand I commit my spirit*: Luke 23:46, from Ps. 31:5 = 6.

167, *sorcerers*: μάγοι has this meaning in Acts 13:6–8.

167, *We all have equal wisdom*: Byron Katie, *A Mind at Home with Itself*, 229.

169, *Everyday mind is the Way*:

> *Wu-men Kuan (The Gateless Barrier)*, 19.

> When Chao-chou was a young student, he asked Zen Master Nan-ch'üan, "What is the Tao?"
>
> The Master said, "Everyday mind is the Tao."
>
> Chao-chou said, "How can I approach it?"
>
> The Master said, "The more you try to approach it, the farther away you'll be."
>
> "But if I don't get close, how can I understand it?"
>
> The Master said, "It's not a question of understanding or not understanding. Understanding is delusion; not understanding is indifference. But when you reach the unattainable Tao, it is like pure space, limitless and serene. Where is there room in it for yes or no?"
>
> At these words, Chao-chou was suddenly enlightened.

174, *The cherubim with their calf's feet*: Ezek. 1:10.

174, *they cover them with two of their wings*: Isa. 6:2.

174, *Balaam*: Num. 22:5–35.

179, *He will be riding upon a donkey*: Zech. 9:9. Matthew gets this wrong: "[Jesus said] to them, "Go into the village ahead of you. Right away you will find a donkey tied there, and a colt beside her. Untie them and bring them to me…. They brought the donkey and the colt and placed their cloaks on them, and he sat on them." Matt. 21:2,7. But John understands: "Jesus found a young donkey and sat on it, as it is written…." John 12:14.

180, *slew a man for wounding him*: Gen. 4:23.

187, *holly, mistletoe, red berries*: Charles Dickens, *A Christmas Carol*, London: Chapman and Hall, 1843, 80.

189–192, *From Luke's story*: Luke 1:26–35, 37–38, 2:1–20. The tendentious Elizabeth episode (Luke 1:5–25, 39–79) is derived from pre-Lucan material and is certainly nonhistorical. One of its intentions in making John the Baptist Jesus's cousin is to subordinate him to Jesus. "This latter detail is never suggested anywhere else in the four Gospels, and is very difficult [more honestly: "impossible"—SM] to reconcile with John 1:33, where John the Baptist says that he didn't even know Jesus … Historically, Jesus was baptized by John and may have gone so far in identifying himself with John's movement as to have become temporarily a disciple of John's." Brown, *The Birth of the Messiah*, 283–85.

193–94, *From Matthew's story*: Matt. 1:18–21, 24–25, 2:1, 9–11, 12b. I have omitted the episodes of the flight to Egypt and the massacre at Bethlehem, which form a separable pre-Matthean narrative. See Brown, *The Birth of the Messiah*, 191–96. "There are serious reasons for thinking that the flight to Egypt and the massacre at Bethlehem may not be historical," Brown, *op. cit.*, 227. In more straightforward words: there is not the slightest reason to think that these events are historical; they are myth. In any case, "a journey to Egypt is quite irreconcilable with Luke's account of an orderly and uneventful return from Bethlehem to Nazareth shortly after the birth of the child." Brown, *op. cit.*, 225.

Acknowledgments

Among the many books on the Nativity that I consulted, the most helpful was Raymond E. Brown's *The Birth of the Messiah*, a masterful study in spite of its Catholic biases.

I want to express my gratitude to Linda Loewenthal, my agent, for her steadfast confidence in this book. I am also grateful to my editor, Joel Fotinos, whose request to hear more of my authorial voice resulted in the interludes and epilogue. Thank you, Joel, for making this a better book. Thanks are also due to the excellent staff at St. Martin's Press.